'I'd better go  easy to do so here.'

Lucinda gave a little grumble and laid her head on his chest. Seb was right; she knew they shouldn't make love, not here and not so soon, but her resistance around this man was practically zero.

'Like what?' she said huskily, not wanting the evening to end, but his answer to her seductive question came as such a surprise for once she was completely lost for words.

'Like fall in love.' He gently kissed the top of her head. 'I'd better get back.' Dumbly she nodded, and stood quite still as he left. He felt it too; it wasn't just her! How on earth, she wondered, was she supposed to sleep after that?

Carol Marinelli did her nursing training in England and then worked for a number of years in Casualty. A holiday romance while backpacking led to her marriage and emigration to Australia. Eight years and three children later the romance continues...

Today she considers both England and Australia her home. The sudden death of her father prompted a reappraisal of her life's goals and inspired her to tackle romance-writing seriously.

Recent titles by the same author:

THE OUTBACK NURSE

DR CARLISLE'S CHILD

BY

CAROL MARINELLI

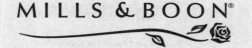

MILLS & BOON®

For Mario.
With love and gratitude for all your support.

*MILLS & BOON and MILLS & BOON with the Rose Device
are registered trademarks of the publisher.*

*First published in Great Britain 2001
Harlequin Mills & Boon Limited,
Eton House, 18-24 Paradise Road, Richmond, Surrey TW9 1SR*

© Carol Marinelli 2001

ISBN 0 263 82702 X

*Set in Times Roman 10½ on 12 pt.
03-1101-52071*

*Printed and bound in Spain
by Litografia Rosés, S.A., Barcelona*

CHAPTER ONE

ALL eyes were on Lucinda Chambers as she walked onto the paediatric cardiac unit at Melbourne Central Women's and Children's Hospital, and she knew it. Pushing her shoulders back, she assumed what she hoped was a confident poise and, reminding herself to breathe, she made her way over to the group of white coats huddled around the nurses' station.

'Ah, Miss Chambers.' Professor Hays held out his hand and Lucinda accepted his handshake firmly. 'I trust you had a pleasant flight.' Without waiting for her reply, he turned and addressed his loyal followers. 'As you know, Miss Chambers joins us today from Queensland, bringing with her a wealth of knowledge and talent from which we can all benefit. As you know, until Mr Felix returns from overseas Miss Chambers will be the only consultant on my team so I am, of course, counting on you all to give her every assistance.' He paused for a moment as the group murmured their agreement.

Lucinda smiled back at the faces, some curious, others indifferent and a couple downright hostile. Her appointment as Consultant Paediatric Cardiothoracic Surgeon had caused more than a few raised eyebrows. At thirty-four she was considered young for such a senior position and a woman to boot. Cardiothoracic surgery was still predominantly male-dominated, even in these so-called liberated times. For a woman to make it in this field took more than just talent with a scalpel.

But, then, Lucinda had it all—good-looking by any standards, with long thick hair, an exquisite shade of chestnut, flawless creamy skin and a curvaceous, supple body that belied the never-ending take-aways, hospital canteen food and diet Coke that she survived on.

More relevantly, she also happened to be the daughter of two of Queensland's most prominent cosmetic surgeons who were ambitious in the extreme where their daughter was concerned. Her mother, despite being possibly the least maternal woman ever to give birth, had been almost pathological in her desire for her daughter's success, planning her education and career almost from the moment of conception.

Though confident she had got the job on her own merits, Lucinda acknowledged that her breeding hadn't been a hindrance. The fact that there were a couple of noses out of joint amongst her new colleagues came as no particular surprise.

'Well, enough of the introductions for now. We'll get started on the ward round, but there will be a small luncheon in the function room at noon so we can welcome Miss Chambers properly. I hope to see you all there.'

As the charge nurse wheeled a large trolley containing the patients' files and X-rays, the group followed. Professor Hays was leading, of course, with the charge nurse to his left and slightly behind. Lucinda assumed her position just to his right and slightly back, with the rest of the procession bringing up the rear in order of merit. It was old-school and had probably been abandoned years ago on most other wards, but Professor Hays was a stickler for formality.

'A small speech would go down well at lunchtime,' he said in low tones to Lucinda. 'To introduce yourself. Just a few words, very informal, nothing to worry about.'

'I'd be glad to,' Lucinda replied confidently as her stomach turned 360 degrees. The thought of facing that adverse group did nothing to inspire her. The charge nurse turned and gave her an almost imperceptible wink and Lucinda winked back. Looking at her name badge, she saw that her name was Ann Benton. Her face, apart from Professor Hays's, had been the only friendly one she had seen so far. For the first time that day Lucinda's smile was genuine.

'First we have young Billy Carlisle.' Ann introduced the young boy sitting cross-legged on his bed, clutching a large unfriendly-looking robot.

'Mr Hughes, perhaps you'd like to brief Miss Chambers and the students on Billy's condition?'

Pete cleared his throat and spoke in the low tones, which enabled the staff to hear but not the patient.

'Billy Carlisle, five years old. Born by emergency C-section at thirty-five weeks gestation due to premature labour with malpresentation and foetal distress. At birth a heart murmur was noticed and subsequent testing showed a large ventricular septal defect.'

Lucinda glanced over to the bed at the young boy trying to get his mother's attention as she filed her nails. Her heart skipped a beat. He was easily the cutest child she had ever seen. Raven curls framed his pale face, his lips were full and tinged with blue yet Lucinda just knew that once he had the surgery to correct the cardiac defect he'd been born with they would be a dark red. His eyes were a vivid green. Glancing up, he caught her staring and gave her a cheeky smile.

For a second she froze, about to look away in her usual fashion, but for some reason she couldn't explain Lucinda found herself smiling back.

Pete Hughes continued with his speech and Lucinda tore her eyes away from the young boy and forced herself to concentrate.

'We were initially hoping to avoid surgery but his condition has started to deteriorate due to development of an associated atrial septal defect. As you can see, he's cyanosed and is having trouble keeping up with his peers. Billy also suffers from chronic asthma, which currently is proving difficult to control and is exacerbating his cardiac problems. He's scheduled for Theatre on Wednesday.'

The entourage moved closer around Billy's bedside, and a couple of students stood with their stethoscopes poised as Billy resignedly undid his pyjama top and let them listen to his chest.

'Good morning, Gemma.' Professor Hays greeted the child's mother in a surprisingly familiar fashion.

'Is it?' she barked rudely. 'Seb was supposed to be here an hour ago. I've got an appointment in the City at ten.'

'Seb's still in Theatre. I know Casualty had a couple of urgent cases this morning—he shouldn't be too much longer,' Professor Hays answered soothingly. So that was why he was being so familiar. Her husband must be a doctor here. Professor Hays turned to Lucinda.

'Young Billy's father is Sebastian Carlisle, one of our consultant anaesthetists,' he explained to Lucinda. 'An excellent anaesthetist—I know you'll enjoy working with him,' he said in a booming voice, then added in quieter tones, 'He talks to his patients while they're under, mind. I've never quite worked him out.'

'Well, I've got some forms I need him to sign before I go. Can't somebody page him?' Gemma asked petulantly.

'And for a second I thought she was here for her son,' Ann muttered darkly into Lucinda's ear, then, smiling brightly, she turned to the agitated woman. 'No worries, Gemma, I'll have someone do that now,' she said, nodding to the ward clerk as she spoke. 'Was there anything you wanted to ask Professor Hays about Billy?'

Gemma frowned slightly. 'Seb deals with all the medical side of things.'

Ann ruffled Billy's hair. 'I'll be back to you later, sport. You can choose this morning's video.'

His eyes widened. 'Can I? Then I want—'

'*Robot Savers*!' said Ann, Professor Hays, Pete Hughes, a couple of other doctors and all the nursing staff in unison. The only one who didn't join in the fun was his mother, who looked pointedly at her watch.

'How did we guess?' Ann laughed. Lucinda had no idea what they were talking about but she again found herself smiling at the cheeky little scamp who had everyone wrapped around his finger. Everyone that was, except his mother.

Gemma stood up. 'About time,' she said pointedly as the ward doors opened and a doctor dressed in theatre greens entered. Lucinda felt her stomach muscles tighten. There could be no doubt it was Billy's father. He had the same vivid green eyes and the same raven curls, but with just a sprinkling of silver which gave him a certain air of distinction. His height and build increased his air of authority. Standing well over six feet, even in his baggy theatre gear one couldn't help but notice his athletic physique. Now, Sebastian Carlisle was most definitely her type, but married, Lucinda reminded herself. Wasn't it always the way? All the decent men, it seemed, were already spoken for.

Sebastian Carlisle pointedly ignored his wife's acid remarks as he made his way to his son's bedside, his haughty face softening as he kissed Billy.

'I was on my way over when you paged me.' He nodded politely to the professor. 'Is everything all right?'

'No, everything is not all right,' Gemma rudely interrupted Professor Hays's assurances. 'I have an appointment at ten and you know I needed to talk to you this morning.'

Sebastian seemed unfazed by the argumentative tones of his wife.

'And you know that I'm a doctor. I can't just walk out halfway through an operation. Anyway, I'm here now.'

The staff had started to move on to the next bed but Lucinda noted that Billy's respiration rate was increasing and he was starting to use his accessory muscles. 'Ann, when did Billy last have a nebuliser?'

'An hour ago.'

Gently Lucinda sat the young boy forward and, lifting his pyjama top, listened to his chest.

'He's a bit tight. Give him another 2.5 mg of Ventolin.' She checked his drug chart. 'He's got a PRN order.' Lucinda turned to Jack Wells, the junior intern. 'Have a listen to his chest later on, he might need his medication reviewed again.'

Jack nodded, blushing when she addressed him, and hastily scribbled Lucinda's orders into the notebook he was carrying as they moved on to the next bed.

'Good morning, Bianca, and how are we feeling?' Professor Hays's cheerful, booming greeting seemed a ridiculous contrast to the young painfully thin girl lying exhausted against her mountain of pillows. Yet somehow the frail teenager summoned up the strength to remove her oxygen mask and give the professor a thumbs-up sign.

'Good,' she gasped. 'And you, Prof?'

He laughed heartily. 'Oh, you know me—in a rush as always.'

Bianca said something but the words were inaudible as she coughed and struggled for breath. Ann, however, used to the young girl, leant over the bed and translated for the benefit of the entourage. 'What time's tee-off?'

Everyone laughed, yet Lucinda knew it was tinged with sadness and that the fragile form on the bed, laughing and joking with the professor like a school pal in the playground, was more than just a patient to the staff here.

Professor Hays turned his back on Bianca and spoke in low tones to Lucinda, but before he even started to talk she had guessed the diagnosis.

'Bianca Moore, thirteen years old, end-stage cystic fibrosis. She's on the waiting list for a double lung and heart transplant. She's held her own for a long time, but in the last fortnight her condition has started to deteriorate rapidly.'

Ann put up the latest chest x-rays. The group gathered round and studied the films as Professor Hays went into greater detail about Bianca's condition. Lucinda listened as she flicked through Bianca's blood results.

'Her potassium's high,' she stated.

'We're aware of that and it's being corrected. She's been given Resonium,' Pete Hughes answered smartly, his casual voice belying the menacing look in his eyes. Lucinda could almost taste the animosity. Professor Hays said nothing, but Lucinda could feel his scrutiny and knew only too well he was assessing how she dealt with her new status.

'Which is the right treatment, of course,' Lucinda answered calmly. 'But her potassium isn't just slightly raised—it's dangerously high. Shouldn't she be on a cardiac monitor?'

Pete Hughes threw her a look of utter contempt but his voice conveyed the same friendly tones. 'I think she's on enough monitors, don't you? I spoke with Bianca and she got very distressed. She likes to get up and have a shower. She's on all the right treatment—it should be resolved by this evening.'

Lucinda understood his judgement, far more than he realised. The child had been through enough. A cardiac monitor curtailed the few privileges that Bianca had left, like a

morning shower. Yet she also knew he was letting his in-
volvement with the patient cloud his judgement. They
weren't here to make friends. They were here to save lives,
and if Bianca was going to be upset by a cardiac monitor
then so be it. Better that than have a child who had already
been through so much die from something as preventable
as a cardiac arrhythmia caused by a raised potassium level
that they were aware of.

'I'd like Bianca on a cardiac monitor, please.' She turned
to Ann, who nodded and wrote the order on a pad.

'Now, if that's possible.'

Ann smiled warmly. 'No worries.' Turning to a junior
colleague Ann relayed her message and in seconds a cardiac monitor appeared by the grumbling Bianca's bedside.

'It will probably come off tonight,' Lucinda said firmly,
knowing a day was a lifetime to this child.

Ann sat her up and deftly placed the red dots that would
hold the monitors' leads onto Bianca's chest. The upright
motion allowed an increase in the air entry into her damaged lungs, giving more clarity to her feeble voice.

'What's your name?' she demanded. Lucinda kept her
feet firmly planted on the floor and her shoulders back.

'Miss Chambers.' She heard the unanimous intake of
breath from her colleagues at her obvious distancing from
the patient. The only person who didn't seem offended was
Bianca.

'You're not very friendly, are you?' she stated matter-
of-factly.

Lucinda approached her bedside and leant over, her face
inches away from Bianca, beckoning her as if to share a
secret. 'I might not be very friendly,' she whispered into
her ear just loudly enough for everyone to hear, 'but I'm a
great doctor.' Pleasingly, her words seemed to appease
Bianca and the young girl gave Lucinda a weak thumbs-

up sign, a gesture that at this stage Lucinda didn't know how much she would come to cherish.

Her reputation as hard had obviously followed her from Queensland, but it didn't concern Lucinda. She had learned long ago that in her line of work emotions and cardiothoracic surgery simply didn't mix. She had lost count of the times she had cried into her pillow at night over a young life lost, until finally the only way for her to cope had been to erect the barriers and retain a cool distance.

The round took ages. Once they had finished with the cardiac unit they made their way along the hospital corridor, losing Jack Wells *en route* when he was paged to return there and Pete Hughes who was urgently needed in Casualty.

Somewhat depleted, they arrived on NICU, the neonatal intensive care unit, to see pre- and post-operative patients. Here, more than anywhere, lives hung precariously in the balance, the lives of tiny babies whose conditions were monitored second by second by the dedicated and highly skilled nursing staff, who knew that even the smallest variance could indicate imminent disaster for their fragile charges. Lucinda looked into the incubators at the little scraps fighting for survival against all the odds. The constant beeping and monitor alarms in the unit was something Lucinda had grown used to by now, but for new parents the whole experience was terrifying.

Sue Washington met them and introduced herself as the charge nurse.

'I'm sorry, Andrew's busy, so you'll have to put up with me taking you around.'

Professor Hays motioned his acceptance and the round commenced.

'Andrew Doran is the neonatologist here,' Sue explained.

'You'll meet him in a few moments—he's actually with one of your patients, a micro-prem.'

'How many weeks' gestation?' Lucinda asked.

'Twenty-four weeks,'

Lucinda's grimace didn't go unnoticed. 'And the fact she's one of ours doesn't sound too promising?' Lucinda ventured.

Sue gave her a knowing a look. 'Exactly. Kimberley Stewart was born with nearly every problem in the book, and what she wasn't born with she's collected along the way. She went back to Theatre last night with necrotising enterocolitis. I can safely say that at the moment her cardiac defect is the least of her problems, so you can hazard a guess at how sick she is.'

Jack Wells, somewhat breathless, appeared, notebook poised, his face even redder than before. 'Sorry, sir, I got held up with Billy Carlisle.'

Professor Hays frowned. 'How's his chest?'

'Fine now but I had to give him a further neb. His asthma worsens every time his mother leaves and now Gemma is demanding that he be moved to a side ward. That's the last thing he needs but try telling it to that awful woman.'

'That's enough, Dr Wells,' Professor Hays said sharply. 'You don't know all the circumstances.'

Jack Wells's face was practically purple now, and Lucinda could tell he was angry.

'I know enough to know that she leaves Billy on his own too much already, without him being moved to a side ward. Something needs to be said.'

Lucinda had only met Jack that morning but she could tell his outburst was out of character. Professor Hays seemed to realise this, too, and ignored his junior's insubordination, addressing him this time in a kinder tone.

'I know you're concerned—we all are. Sister Benton has

tried to have a word with Gemma. It's very awkward, with Seb being a doctor here.' Professor Hays then addressed Lucinda. 'Gemma and Seb are divorced,' he explained. 'Mrs Carlisle apparently feels very uncomfortable in the hospital. She assumes that we're all on Seb's side and gets easily upset, which, of course, translates to Billy. It's not doing his asthma any good.'

Lucinda frowned. She really couldn't care less about the Carlisles' marital disputes, but when it affected her patient that was another matter.

'Perhaps I could have a word with them?' Lucinda offered. 'Billy needs to have his parents around at the moment. If I talk to both of them together, lay it on the line so to speak, Mrs Carlisle can hardly accuse me of favouritism.'

'But you'll be working closely with Seb. It's hardly a great start to your working relationship,' Professor Hays pointed out.

Lucinda considered this but only for a moment.

'From all accounts, Sebastian Carlisle is a fine doctor, and shall continue to be whether he likes me or not. I can understand that it's hard for you all to say anything about this, given that you know him personally, but I'm here to treat patients, not to win a personality competition. If Billy's asthma is suffering because of his parents, it needs to be addressed.'

Professor Hays nodded. 'Very well. You're right, of course.' He turned to Jack. 'Are they both still here?'

Jack nodded. 'Gemma's seen the side ward is empty and is demanding that Billy be moved now.'

Professor Hays scratched his bald head. 'Maybe it would be for the best if you did speak to them. I'll finish up here with Jack.'

On the ward an exasperated Ann met Lucinda.

'I'm going to have to move him,' she said angrily. 'I've tried telling Gemma that Billy should be out on the main ward, mixing with the other children. The last thing he needs is to be feeling sorry for himself in a side ward, but she just won't listen to reason. Anyway, I like to keep a side ward free for the really sick ones.'

Lucinda tried to be objective as she scanned Billy's notes. 'She's probably exhausted. She's more than likely worn out from sleeping by Billy's bed, and Seb being stuck in Theatre was probably the last straw.'

Ann scoffed at this. 'Worn out? She only arrived five minutes before the ward round and she only popped in for half an hour yesterday. Poor Seb's run ragged, juggling a theatre list and trying to be both mum and dad.'

'Well, that's his problem and Billy's reaction to it is mine. Don't worry, Ann, I'll speak to them now.'

Lucinda made her way over to the bedside. 'Could I have a word with you both, please, in Sister Benton's office?' She smiled at Billy. 'We won't be long.' She made her way to the office and sat at the desk as the Carlisles entered. Lucinda didn't waste any time with small talk.

'I understand that you want Billy to be moved to a side ward. Can I ask why?'

'I'm happy for him to stay on the main ward,' Seb said evenly. 'It's Gemma that wants him to be moved.'

'Of course you're happy for him to be on the main ward. It's all right for you—everyone loves Seb,' Gemma snapped, and then turned her angry stare on Lucinda. 'I'm the one who has to put up with the hostility from the nurses just because Seb has custody of Billy. I know what they're all saying behind my back. ''There's the woman who walked out on her husband and child.'' They all hate me.'

'I'm sure that's not the case,' Lucinda said calmly, but Gemma was insistent.

'Oh, I'm telling you that's exactly the case. How would you like it, day in day out, stuck here like a sitting duck for all the snide comments, with everyone judging you. You don't know what it's like, having a child with a hole in the heart—' Her voice was rising and Lucinda cut short her protests.

'You're right, I don't know what it's like to have a sick child and, to be honest, I'm not sure how I'd cope. However, the fact of the matter is Billy's asthma is worsening and he needs a parent to stay with him at the moment as much as possible.'

'Its pure attention-seeking.' Gemma said dismissively, as Seb rolled his eyes at her ridiculous comment.

Lucinda's voice remained calm but she felt the hackles of irritation rising.

'Mrs Carlisle, I can assure you Billy's asthma is far more serious than attention-seeking behaviour. There may be a link with you going, but that's related to his anxiety, and anxiety is increasing the frequency and severity of his attacks. Now, personally I feel that the last thing Billy needs is to be moved to a side ward. He's a bright little boy and he knows those wards are used for the really ill children. He's already spent too much of his young life in hospital and, no doubt, he's somewhat anxious about the surgery. The last thing he needs is to feel further isolated. Children need company, even if it's just to have someone in the next bed to grumble to about the lunchtime shepherd's pie.'

Gemma started to protest but Lucinda put her hand up to halt the woman and continued authoritatively, 'However, if by moving him it means that you feel more comfortable and are prepared to stay around a lot more, well, then, I agree that would be a valid reason for him to be moved to a side ward.'

Gemma opened her mouth to speak but Lucinda still hadn't finished.

'At the moment I understand that you're still on call?' She looked at Seb who nodded at her question.

'Which means that you can't guarantee being around all the time.'

'I'm off roster when he has his operation,' Seb said. 'I'll be able to stay then.'

Lucinda nodded curtly, trying to ignore the unsettling effect his deep voice was having on her.

'Well, Mrs Carlisle, think about it. Whatever you decide, though, I'll have a word with the nursing staff. I would hope that you're mistaken, but if there's any truth to your feelings of hostility from the staff it needs to be addressed. You've got enough on your plate at the moment without it being added to unnecessarily.'

Gemma looked at her, surprised, as if the last thing she'd expected had been someone to come down on her side. 'I'm not imagining it.'

'Then I'll speak to them.'

'Thank you,' she said, somewhat appeased.

'But I would still like you to think about what I've said. I really think Billy will do better out on the main ward, but I'll leave the decision to you.'

'I'll think about it,' she grudgingly agreed, and then turned to Seb. 'I'm going to pop down to the canteen for a coffee. I'll let you know what I decide.'

Seb gave her a tight smile. 'Sure, Gemma.'

'Thanks for that,' he said once Gemma had gone, turning those gorgeous green eyes on Lucinda. 'Ten minutes ago she was all set to move the bed in there herself. Now at least she's thinking about it.'

'I wasn't aware, until Gemma mentioned it, that you have full custody of Billy. It must be hard.'

Seb gave a thin smile but he wasn't giving anything away. 'It can be, but the good times far outweigh the bad.' He quickly changed the subject. 'Gemma does have a point, though. As much as I think we've got the best nursing staff in the world here, they are noticeably cool towards her. Not only is she saddled with the reputation of walking out on her family, she's also been thrown into my environment and, fair or not, the staff tend to come down on my side. Unfortunately everyone has an opinion on the subject.'

Lucinda thought about this. She was also somewhat surprised by Seb's ability to be fair to his ex-wife, who even with the best will in the world was not the most likeable of people.

'Well, they'll have to learn to keep it to themselves,' she said firmly. 'They're here to look after not just Billy but the whole family. Gemma deserves the same respect as you.'

'I agree.'

Lucinda softened a little. He really did seem to be trying hard in these very difficult circumstances. 'Can't you take some annual leave, stay with Billy a bit more?' she said in kinder voice.

Seb shook his head. 'I'm already in the red with my annual leave. I asked to go on compassionate leave, but half the anaesthetic department has come down with flu so they can't let me go till the operation and even then it will only be for a couple of weeks. We had a necrotising enterocolitis and a ruptured appendix last night while the on-call had an emergency thoracotomy. What am I supposed to do then? You can see for yourself how keen Gemma is to stay.'

Lucinda pondered for a moment but they both knew there was no easy solution.

'I'm sorry if I came on a bit strong, but something had to be said.'

Seb waved his hand. 'You really don't have to apologise. You were quite right to say something. I'd have done exactly the same. Hopefully Gemma will take heed.'

He smiled and for a moment his face had the same cheeky look as his son's, but the effect was somewhat more disturbing.

'Well, Miss Chambers, I'm sorry we had to meet in these circumstances, but I've heard a lot of good things about you and I'm looking forward to working with you.' He held out his hand and Lucinda shook it, noticing the firmness of his grip. 'Now, if you'll excuse me, I'd better get back to Billy.'

'Of course.'

As Seb left the room Ann entered.

'How did it go?'

Lucinda shrugged. 'I'm not sure if Gemma will change her mind but Dr Carlisle seemed very amicable.'

'I could think of a few words other than "amicable" to describe him. He's gorgeous, isn't he?' she said saucily.

Lucinda didn't respond. Ann, happy-go-lucky, middle-aged and with a wedding ring on her finger, could make comments like that and get away with it. For Lucinda, however, that type of talk could only lead to gossip and innuendo.

'Gemma did say she felt some hostility coming from the nursing staff.' Lucinda watched as Ann puffed up, on the defensive, but Lucinda carried on talking. 'And I can understand why. You're obviously all fond of Seb but, Ann, it has to stop. Gemma is Billy's mother, and the staff have to forget that his father is Seb. Now, I don't know all the circumstances of the break-up, but I can also be pretty sure that the rest of the staff don't know them either, and certainly not from Gemma's viewpoint. I think it might be prudent for you to have a word, Ann, just to be sure.'

Ann gave a grudging nod. 'You're probably right. I'll speak to them now. We're all a bit guilty, I guess. It's hard to be objective…'

'Well, you'll all just have to try harder, for Billy's sake,' Lucinda retorted, and Ann nodded sheepishly.

'Fair point.'

'I'd better be going. I was supposed to be in Admin half an hour ago. Let me know if there's any more problems with the Carlisles'.

Making her way out of the ward, she noticed Seb and Billy playing happily with a board game. Billy was laughing, with no hint of breathlessness now, as Seb lounged on the bed beside him. Ann was right. Sebastian Carlisle *was* gorgeous, that was undeniable. But he also had a five-year-old son and a wife from hell—or rather an ex-wife, she corrected herself, trying to ignore the sense of relief that thought gave her.

CHAPTER TWO

BY THE time Lucinda had been photographed for her security pass and had filled in a mountain of forms, the morning had disappeared and any hope of preparing a speech for her welcoming luncheon were gone.

In view of her seniority, the catering department had prepared a sumptuous array of finger food with not a single polystyrene cup or paper plate in sight. However, like Lucinda, for most of the senior staff attending, the lunch was a formality and not a pleasure. Professor Hays was the one exception. His glowing speech and obvious delight at having her on board made Lucinda inwardly cringe, but she smiled and shook his hand as he welcomed her onto the platform to address her new colleagues.

The polite but somewhat forced applause did nothing to quell her nerves; neither did the openly hostile look Pete Hughes was throwing her. Andrew Doran looked at his watch, wanting to get back to his babies. Seb, now dressed in a suit, fiddled with his tie, no doubt anxious to return to his son's bedside.

'I know we're all busy people so I'll make this brief.' Her voice was clear and steady, and she stood straight, her white coat discarded for the luncheon.

She wore a cream cashmere dress that clung becomingly to her curvaceous figure; her dark hair, thick and glossy, rippled over her shoulders. Lucinda, in fact, looked like a woman who had spent hours getting ready for this moment. In truth, that morning she had jumped under the shower and spent a mere five minutes blow-drying her long hair and about half that again to add just a touch of eyeliner and lipstick. Her complexion was so clear there was no need for foundation or blusher. Lucinda's looks entirely spoke for themselves.

Her clothes were ludicrously expensive and well tailored, but even that was with reason. With her impossible schedule, she had little or no time for clothes-shopping, so twice a year she set aside a day for what she considered a tiresome necessity, not a luxury, and purchased a select few pieces that would last and look smart. Not one person in the room could have guessed at her apprehension.

'Firstly, I'd like to thank Professor Hays for his words of welcome and for giving me the opportunity to work with him in such a prestigious hospital. I have no doubt I shall learn a lot.

'While I'm proud to be here, I think it's very important to remember that were it not for other people's misfortunes there would be no Melbourne Central, and hence no need for us. So on that note I'll thank you all for coming to welcome me on board and let you get back to the people that really matter—the patients.'

'Hear, hear,' somebody quipped as everyone started clapping, and this time the applause was genuine. Several people came up and shook her hand as she left the platform and congratulated her.

'Nice speech, direct and to the point, like this morning.'

Lucinda swung around at the deep, familiar voice. Seb's green eyes were smiling at her now and Lucinda reluctantly recalled Ann's words.

'That's me,' she said lightly, then added, 'How's Billy?'

'He's settled now, and still out on the main ward, thanks to you. It's their rest time so I thought I'd come and welcome the new consultant as we got off to a rather bad start this morning.'

Lucinda smiled. 'It must be hard, having your son as a patient in the same hospital you work at.'

'Absolutely. Every emergency page I hear sends me into a cold sweat in case it might be Billy, and while it's nice that I can pop down and see him between patients, it's rather embarrassing to have all your dirty washing aired in public.'

Lucinda waited for him to elaborate but he'd obviously said all he was going to on the subject. She stood there uncomfortably, desperately trying to think of something to say. Despite her excellence at public speaking and confidence when discussing medical matters, once on a more social level Lucinda invariably found herself feeling awkward.

After a moment's silence it was Seb who spoke again. 'Pete Hughes looks as if he's at a funeral,' he observed.

'I think he'd like it to be mine.'

Seb gave her a wry smile. 'All's fair in love and promotion. He'll get over it.'

Lucinda's eyes widened. 'So that's his problem? I wish Professor Hays had warned me. I had no idea he was in the running.'

Seb shrugged dismissively. 'He never was. Pete just liked to think he stood a chance. He likes to party a bit too hard for the prof's liking. Much as Professor Hays might look a bit dotty at times, he knows exactly what goes on. Pete's going to need to do a lot more spadework before he wins him over. Anyway, enough about work. How are you settling in Melbourne? Have you found somewhere to live yet?'

She knew he was probably just being polite, but under his steady gaze Lucinda couldn't help but feel that Seb's interest was genuine and she found herself answering back in a softer, less businesslike tone.

'I only arrived on Saturday morning, but I'm starting to find my way around. I found somewhere to live before I came, thank goodness. Admin finally gave me my roster this morning—it wouldn't have left much time for house-hunting.'

'Tell me about it,' he groaned. 'So where are you living?'

'At Southbank, the new apartment complex.'

Seb let out a low whistle. 'They look pretty plush, I saw the advertisements for them. They'd be handy for work, too.'

Lucinda nodded. 'Five minutes away. How about you?'

'Nothing so flash, or near, I'm afraid. I'm more the ''renovator's delight'' type, not that I ever seem to find the time to renovate. Mind you, that can have its advantages when you've got children. Billy may be past the scribbling-on-walls stage, but footballs hurtling through the air and remote-control cars crashing into the plasterwork aren't the best recipe for a luxury home—not that you'd know about that sort of thing,' he added.

Lucinda laughed. 'Actually, I do know what you mean. I've got a godson in Sydney—'

'Miss Chambers, sorry to interrupt.' Professor Hays smiled broadly, looking anything but sorry, and Lucinda's sentence was left unfinished. Seb gave her a slightly questioning look but there was no chance to complete the conversation as the professor had other plans.

'Its nearly time to head over to NICU. Mr Doran wants us there to discuss one of the infants,' Professor Hays explained to Seb. 'Fabulous speech, don't you think? It doesn't do any harm to be reminded who we're here for. I think Miss Chambers is going to be a real asset, don't you agree, Dr Carlisle?'

Seb nodded in agreement and, turning back to Lucinda,

for a second his gaze flickered downwards, his eyes travelling briefly over her body. Lucinda felt her heart rate quicken.

'Absolutely,' Seb replied, his voice deep and rich. 'A real asset.' Replacing his empty glass on the table, he excused himself and left. For a split second Lucinda had the craziest notion to run after him. To tap on his shoulder and explain that what she'd been trying to say had been that she'd moved into her friend's house whilst she'd been on a placement and had seen at first hand the destruction a toddler could cause. That she wasn't so shallow as to think a godson in any way gave her an insight into parenthood. But, of course, she didn't. What would be the point? she reasoned. Sebastian Carlisle had, after all, only been there today to be polite. He'd probably forgotten their conversation as soon as he'd walked out of the door. So why couldn't she just forget it? Lucinda wondered as she joined the professor and walked along the corridor towards NICU, for all the world appearing to listen intently as Professor Hays spoke. Why couldn't she?

Walking along Southbank, the delicious fragrant aroma of the Suriyan Indian Restaurant was just too good to ignore.

'Lovely to see you again, Doctor. You took the job, I gather?'

Lucinda smiled at the greeting, touched Vijay had remembered her.

'Your delectable butter chicken was a very favourable deciding factor. I think we'll be seeing a lot of each other. I'll have it to go tonight, though.' Her friendly remark wasn't untrue. Southbank, set along Melbourne's Yarra River, with its multitude of shops, restaurants and food court all open until late into the night, meant that she would never have to worry about cooking. Not that she didn't enjoy it but the ridiculous hours she worked hardly left enough time for shopping, let alone preparing meals. This cultural melting pot set in such beautiful surroundings offered her a different choice every night, but Indian food was definitely a favourite.

Vijay handed her a card. 'You ring me before you leave the hospital and I'll have your order waiting, no worries. If you're on call, my son will come and deliver to you,' he said in his Indian accent, peppered with Australianisms. 'I know how hard you doctors work. You see my son?' Vijay pointed to a strapping teenager setting up the restaurant tables. 'He was no bigger than this…' Holding up his hands, Vijay showed such an impossibly tiny gap between them that Lucinda knew, unless his son was a medical marvel that even she hadn't heard about, Vijay was exaggerating, but she didn't spoil the story, enjoying the light-hearted banter. 'But when you see him now, such a fine young boy… Your hospital makes many miracles.'

'Do you want a garlic naan?' he added more as an afterthought.

Lucinda shook her head. 'Not very fair on the patients. What was that lovely bread I had last time, with fruit and nuts?'

'Ah, my sweet mincemeat naan. Very good choice, Doctor. And how about some beautiful saffron rice to go with your chicken?'

How could she refuse?

Minutes later Lucinda nodded briefly to the doorman as he pressed the lift button for her. Letting herself into her twentieth-floor apartment, Lucinda set the white plastic bag containing her dinner onto the gleaming benchtop. The cleaner had obviously been in as the morning's breakfast dishes and discarded clothes were all back in their various cupboards, making the place look more like a sterile hotel room than ever.

Her mother had organised the apartment for her through a real-estate contact, and while it was sumptuous, with glittering bay and city views shimmering through the full-length windows, it didn't do much for Lucinda.

Kicking off her cream suede shoes, she wiggled her toes luxuriously in the thick white carpet. White everything really, she noted, except for the black granite benchtops and stainless-steel appliances. Yes, it was luxurious, but hardly homely. There was nothing remotely personal about it. Still, she could set about finding somewhere more to her taste in a few months when she had the job under control.

Checking the answering machine, Lucinda couldn't help but feel a stab of disappointment that her parents hadn't rung to see how her first day had gone. Then she checked herself. What did she expect? Instead, there were a couple of boring messages, one from her new bank, the other from the caretaker of the apartment block warning her of a fire-alarm check. She toyed with the idea of ringing her parents, but what was the point? They were probably out at some restaurant.

Instead, she put the foil cartons into the cooker, set it on low and then ran a deep bath. Slipping into the water, she closed her eyes, resting her head back as she reflected on her first day as a consultant. It had taken a lot to get here, so why now, she wondered, when she was at the top, or at least very near, didn't she feel happier? Why wasn't she lying in the bath in this marble bathroom with a self-satisfied grin and a glow of achievement?

Because there was no one to share it with. Lucinda tried to ignore the thought and pulled out the plug, wrapping herself in a huge bathrobe, but that inner voice wouldn't go away. Because for all your talk and bravado, you're not that hard and you do care.

Listlessly she served up her dinner and, carrying the plate

over to the sofa, took in the gorgeous sunset. The whole of Melbourne lay before her, the bay shimmering gold. It was a view made for sharing.

For a second Lucinda felt so lonely it hurt. She had never had a problem attracting the opposite sex, and was never short of offers for dates. But her relationships, if you could call them that, never seemed to get anywhere. Men didn't like playing second fiddle to her career and the gloss soon wore off for her, too. Maybe she set her sights too high? But what was wrong with that? She wanted to get it right the first time. Imagine ending up like Sebastian and Gemma Carlisle? What a mess. Casting her mind back, she remembered the way Seb had looked at her at the luncheon.

'A real asset,' he'd said, but it was the *way* he'd said it. Lucinda felt her stomach tighten just at the memory of his voice. Sebastian Carlisle was gorgeous, disturbingly so, but completely out of bounds, of course. Lucinda didn't have a hard-and-fast rule about not mixing business with pleasure, but on the whole avoided it. Who needed the complication? Anyway, on Wednesday she would be operating with Professor Hays on his *son*. The word was a sobering thought.

Covered by the green sterile theatre drapes and with a multitude of wires, tubes and monitors attached to his body, the small form lying on the operating table was unrecognisable as Billy. But there was an increased air of tension in the theatre that morning as all of the staff worked alongside and knew Sebastian Carlisle well. The fact it was Seb's son lying there didn't mean Billy would get better treatment—all the young patients were afforded the best possible care. But it did mean that each staff member had a personal stake in this operation for they had all heard about

Billy and his setbacks and achievements relayed in Seb's deep drawl over the past five years.

For Lucinda, however, the emotions that ran through her when the boy was prepared with a Betadine solution and a large occlusive dressing placed over the site of incision to reduce his chances of infection came as a total surprise. Her air of tension had nothing to do with the fact his father was an anaesthetist at the hospital. This morning it was all to do with Billy.

When she had popped into the ward that morning for the pre-op round he had again given her the benefit of that cheeky smile and she'd felt her hardened heart melt slightly. She'd smiled back at him and, more amazingly, had stopped to listen when Billy had turned his robot on for her benefit, watching as the metallic figure had clunked around his bedside table. Gemma had been nowhere to be seen, but Seb had been there, smiling appreciatively at her for taking the time to indulge Billy.

'Thanks for that.' He'd come up to her as she'd left the ward. 'He might seem all right but he's pretty nervous.'

'You, too?'

Seb had nodded. 'I know technically it's a pretty straightforward operation, but that's the medical side of me trying to rationalise things. At the end of the day it keeps coming back to me that it's my son's heart that's being operated on.'

'We'll take good care of him,' she'd said in her most confident voice as she'd stridden off towards the theatres. It was what she said to all the parents but for some reason this time it hadn't seemed enough, and she had been left wishing she could have somehow comforted him more.

But like the rest of the theatre staff, Lucinda put her emotions to one side as the operation commenced and Professor Hays made his incision. Billy's temperature was brought down to reduce his body's demand for oxygen and he was placed onto heart bypass. Professor Hays was indeed a skilled operator and Lucinda's talent complemented his skills. Neither was the type for small talk or background music. They worked in quiet harmony, with only the occasional exchange of words.

Their attention was completely focused on the small damaged heart until finally, with her back aching, Lucinda sat up on her stool and Professor Hays instructed the perfusionist that Billy was ready to be weaned off the bypass machine. The tension in the room increased again but lifted as the small heart filled with blood and started pumping.

'Good work, everybody. Miss Chambers, I'll leave you to close Master Carlisle and I'll go and speak to his parents, let them know how well it went.'

Lucinda stayed with Billy in the recovery room, writing out the post-operative instructions and ordering the multitude of drugs Billy would be needing, as well as the intravenous fluids orders. For the next twenty-four hours he would be in Intensive Care on a respirator to allow him to rest and to enable the staff to concentrate on his heart. But, all being well, he would then be moved off the intensive care unit and back onto his old ward, but in the four-bedded high-dependency section.

A nurse escorted Seb, Gemma and a woman Lucinda didn't recognise to the gurney where Billy lay. Lucinda stepped away slightly, allowing them nearer. Only Gemma held back.

'Mummy and Daddy are here and Aunty Isabella. Professor Hays said you've been a very brave boy. We're all so proud.' Seb's words were gentle and comforting but Lucinda could hear the break in his voice, could see the tension in his shoulders as he leant over the trolley, his strong brown hands gently caressing his son's face.

'It went very well.' Lucinda said gently to Gemma,

knowing Professor Hays would have said the same thing but realising it was all they would want to hear. 'He's heavily sedated but talk to him, hold his hand.'

Seb turned to his ex-wife. 'Come on, Gemma, hold his hand let him know we're all here for him.' His voice held no malice, just a hint of pleading. Gemma stepped forward and hesitantly picked up one of Billy's pale hands.

'Mummy's here, Billy.' But it was Seb who spoke. Gemma just stood there, frozen. 'Talk to him Gemma, please,' Seb said gruffly.

Gemma replaced Billy's hand on the starched blanket. 'I have to make a phone call. I'll be down in the canteen.'

'Gemma, please,' Seb pleaded, but it fell on deaf ears. Gemma hurriedly left the recovery area.

'Just let her go,' Isabella said wearily.

'Sometimes all the equipment can be a bit intimidating,' the theatre nurse ventured, but Seb said nothing and Lucinda was sure she could see a glint of tears in his vivid eyes as he gently stroked his son's hair. Lucinda carried on writing up the charts, relaying her instructions to the theatre nurse as she wrote them. The nurse would in turn pass on her orders to the intensive care staff.

The porters arrived to wheel the gurney over to Intensive Care.

'We'll get him over now, Dr Carlisle,'

Seb nodded. 'Isabella, will you go and tell Gemma they're moving him? I want to stay around.'

Isabella gave Billy a quick kiss and made her way out of the recovery area as the staff checked and rechecked the oxygen and equipment on the trolley to ensure they were prepared for any eventuality on the short journey across to the unit.

'I'll come and let you know when they're ready for you to see him, Seb,' the theatre nurse said kindly but firmly.

Seb nodded resignedly and Lucinda knew that he wanted more than anything to go with his son, but though he had been allowed into the out-of-bounds theatre recovery area it was better that they settled Billy away from Seb. He wasn't a doctor here, but the child's father.

As the trolley moved off Seb made his way over to the small annexe off the recovery area.

Lucinda watched as he walked off, his face etched with anxiety and his usual air of confidence gone. She had given him the usual spiel on the ward, and it had left her feeling empty. It was time for something more.

Sometimes words did help, but then there were times when knowing when to say nothing helped more. As Lucinda made her way into the annexe she knew it should be Gemma here, that Billy's parents should be comforting and leaning on each other through this terrible angst-filled time. But for some reason Gemma was instead sitting in the canteen, making her calls, leaving Seb to battle with a myriad emotions in that small sterile room.

Lucinda knew there was nothing she could say to help so instead she went and sat quietly beside him. It was a moment or two before Seb acknowledged she was there and when he finally spoke his voice was thick with emotion.

'He's been through so much, poor kid. It's bad enough with all the operations and his asthma, but his mum and dad breaking up as well and now Gemma can't even bear to hold his hand. It's like she doesn't want to even be in the same room with him.' His voice broke. 'How much can one little guy take?' Seb took a couple of deep breaths and sat up straight, embarrassed at betraying so much feeling. 'I'm sorry. You don't need to hear all this,' he said in a gruff voice.

But Lucinda shook her head. 'Please, don't apologise. I know it's awful for all of you.'

Seb continued tentatively as if he had to justify his words. 'It was just so awful to see him like that. More than anyone, I knew what to expect but it was still a shock. The prof told me it went well, told me a bit too much detail really.' He winced. 'There's some things you really don't need to know.'

'I understand,' she said, but the words came out wrong and she almost heard her mother's affected tones in her voice.

Seb turned and gave her a cynical look. 'Ah, yes,' he said dryly. 'After all, you've got a godson.'

Lucinda stiffened. She knew he was hurting but at least she was here, at least she was trying. She stood up smartly. 'I'd better get back.' Her crisp demeanour returned and she made no attempt now to hide it, but Seb was contrite for his sarcastic words and he stood up as well, his hand reaching out and touching her arm as she turned to go.

'That was completely uncalled for. I know you're trying to help.'

Lucinda said nothing. Acutely aware of the warm strength of his hand on her bare arm, she found herself unable to tear her eyes away from his steady gaze. It was Seb who finally broke the spell.

'Thank you,' he said simply. 'Thank you for being here.'

Lucinda nodded. For a moment she was speechless, bewildered by the turbulent thoughts he so easily evoked. Finally she found her voice. 'I really do have to go now.'

They left the annexe together. Seb returned to Billy and Lucinda made her way to the sink where she started the long and tedious process of scrubbing for the next operation. But for both there was a gentle disquiet, a lingering feeling that something special had happened in those few moments. Something good and strong, a tiny foundation from which to build.

CHAPTER THREE

'WE ARE honoured.' Ann Benton looked up from her desk and gave Lucinda a tired smile as she entered the nurse unit manager's office. 'A registrar and a consultant on the ward on a Saturday evening. Is one of my patients sick that I don't know about?'

Lucinda shook her head. 'I hope not! One of the premmies on NICU went into atrial fibrillation. She's kept us all on our toes this afternoon,' Lucinda explained. Little Kimberley's heart had been beating too rapidly and causing a lot of concern. Lucinda had been called in for an emergency consultation and after a multitude of tests and drugs the baby's arrhythmia was starting to settle. 'Who else is here, then?'

'Pete Hughes. He's going out with one of my nurses. We're short tonight and Ellen offered to stay till seven, so Pete's hanging around, otherwise we wouldn't see him for dust.'

Lucinda raised her eyebrows but didn't comment. 'How are my patients—any concerns?' she asked instead.

'You mean, how's Billy? You really have got a soft spot for him, and here was me expecting an ice queen. You're as soft as butter, Miss Chambers.' Ann had an ability to say exactly what everyone was thinking and somehow manage not to cause offence. Lucinda knew all about her own reputation and it was in some way a relief to be able to let down her guard with this likeable, knowledgeable woman.

'Billy's fine. We've taken him out of high dependency this morning and he's back on the general ward now. He'll

probably be going home on Monday or Tuesday, but then
that's up to you, of course. He's already watched his favourite video three times.'

Lucinda gave a small chuckle. 'So he's definitely turned
the corner. Has his mum been in?'

Ann gave a knowing look. 'Yes, she's making the occasional appearance—dressed to the nines with not a hair
out of place, unlike most of the other mums in this place
who hardly manage to pull on a pair of leggings and a
T-shirt and run a comb through their hair. Mrs Carlisle
certainly doesn't let her son's illness curtail her. Hard to
understand, isn't it?' she said glumly. 'He's so cute you
just can't imagine her not wanting to be with him.'

'Ours is not to reason why,' Lucinda said matter-of-
factly, although privately she agreed with every word.

'I know, I just worry for Seb. You were right to say
something about the way the staff were treating Gemma. I
try not to let my feelings for Seb show but, well, we've
been friends for years, and it's hard seeing him go through
the mill. Not that Seb ever complains. As close as we are,
I never really know what he's thinking. He keeps his emotions pretty much under lock and key.'

After Lucinda's reprimand Ann had addressed the ward
staff, making things easier not only for the Carlisles but for
the nursing staff, too. Ann had apologised to Lucinda for
letting things get so out of hand but Lucinda had only been
grateful the problem had been so easily sorted. From this
unsteady beginning a firm friendship was being forged.

'Seb seems to be coping. I mean, I spoke to him after
the operation and he was pretty upset, but any parent would
be.'

Ann gave her a surprised look. 'Seb was upset? In front
of you?'

Lucinda nodded. 'But it's only to be expected. Billy had just had major heart surgery. You seem shocked—why?'

Ann gave a small shrug. 'Like I said, I've known Seb a long time, and I've never seen him with his guard down.'

Lucinda thought for moment. 'Professor Hays apparently went into rather a lot of detail about the procedure. Maybe it was that.'

'Maybe,' Ann replied, but she didn't sound convinced. 'I'm just glad someone was there with him when he was upset.' She gave Lucinda a smile. 'He doesn't deserve to be alone.'

Under Ann's beady eyes Lucinda felt the beginnings of a blush, and she hastily changed the subject—the last thing she needed was Ann to realise she had a crush on Sebastian Carlisle. What would that do to her reputation? 'Any other concerns on the ward?'

Ann gave a worried frown. 'I'm a bit concerned about Bianca Moore. I know she's not strictly your patient until she has her transplant.' Ann automatically touched the wooden desk. 'And let it be soon, please, God. But I can't get hold of the intern. Her parents brought her in a burger and chips and normally she'd wolf it down, but she hasn't touched it, though there's nothing I can put my finger on. For all I go on about Pete Hughes, he's been good enough to look over her notes—that's what he's doing now.'

At that moment Pete walked in. Dressed casually in jeans and a white T-shirt, he still looked immaculate.

'Evening, Lucinda. How's Kimberley?' His comment was professional but the trace of bitterness in his voice didn't go unnoticed by either woman.

'She's had some more Lasix and we've digitalised her. She's not too good, though. How's Bianca?'

Pete placed the file on the desk in front of Ann. 'I've

had a look and she seems fine. Maybe she just wasn't hungry.'

'Thanks for looking anyway.' Ann gave a small shrug but Lucinda could tell she was still worried.

A pretty young nurse knocked on the office door. 'I've handed over my patients to Sister Spencer—they all seem fine. Billy Carlisle is just having another nebuliser.'

'Is his mum there?' Ann asked.

'No, she just left, but his dad's with him. He's going to stay the night again in the doctors' on-call room next door once Billy's asleep. He said to call him any time Billy wakes up.' She smiled at Pete. 'Are you done?'

Pete nodded. 'See you, ladies—hopefully not till Monday,' he added half-jokingly. Lucinda gave a rueful smile. Weekends on call, even as a consultant, were rarely if ever that quiet.

'Was that Kimberley Stewart you were talking about?' Ann asked, pouring two coffees.

Lucinda nodded. 'Do you know the family?'

'No, it's just my nosy nature. She's the micro-prem on NICU, isn't she?' As Lucinda nodded Ann pulled a worried face. 'Any chance she'll make it, I mean realistically?'

Lucinda took a sip of her coffee before she answered. Kimberley and her family had been causing a great deal of anxiety and it was actually nice to be able to talk about it with Ann. 'If she doesn't it won't be for the want of trying, but realistically, no, I don't think there's much hope.'

Ann didn't say anything and Lucinda found herself continuing. 'It's such a shame. Her mother has idiopathic infertility.'

'In English, please,' Ann said. 'I'm on a cardiac ward, remember?'

'There's no reason that can be found as to why she can't get pregnant,' Lucinda explained. 'Apparently they've been trying for years. This pregnancy was after their sixth and final attempt at IVF.'

'Final?' Ann questioned. 'Why?'

'They can't afford to do it any more, either emotionally or financially. Their marriage is under a terrible strain. I went to the team meeting about them, and from what Sue Washington was saying they're hardly talking. Janine, the mother, is completely wrapped up in Kimberley. Mark, the father, has to head back to work on Monday. It's not the ideal situation but Kimberley's seven weeks old now.'

'And the bills don't stop coming in just because you've got a sick child,' Ann added.

'Exactly. The nurses were just telling me it's their wedding anniversary today. Ten years, can you imagine? I don't seem to be able to manage ten weeks in my relationships.'

Ann laughed. 'You just haven't met the right man yet. Tod and I have been together twenty-five years now and I couldn't imagine it any other way.' She thought for a moment 'It's a shame they can't go out for their anniversary, get away from the hospital for a while.'

Lucinda nodded. 'It's a shame all round. Anyway, there's not much I can do about it. I'm a doctor, not a marriage guidance councillor. Who am I to offer advice?' She stood up to go. 'Thanks for the coffee. Do you want me to have a look at Bianca for you before I go? I can tell you're still not happy.'

Ann gave a relieved smile. 'Please. I don't want to go worrying her. She knows more about her condition than us, but I'm sure she's not right.'

Lucinda made her way down the darkened ward. By seven-thirty the lights were down and the children were being settled. There was strange background music coming over the intercom with the sound of running water and birds chirping. Ann had been given some CDs to try out that supposedly relaxed children. Lucinda wondered if she'd be burning incense next!

Seb hadn't made it to the on-call room and lay sound asleep next to Billy, his long legs dangling uncomfortably from the small bed. Billy was held firmly in the crook of his father's muscular arm with his head resting on Seb's broad chest. They looked the picture of contentment. It was hard to believe, seeing them lying there so peacefully, the problems they had both faced.

'You still awake?' Lucinda stood at the side of Bianca's bed. The young girl gave her a suspicious look.

'What are you doing here?'

'Just checking on my patients.'

'Why? You're a consultant. Shouldn't you be at some fancy ball on a Saturday night?'

Lucinda gave a small laugh. 'You make it sound very glamorous. I'm new. I like to make sure of things myself— I'll go home later.' Lucinda looked at the take-away cartons. 'Didn't fancy your burger, huh?'

Bianca shook her head. 'No, but I'm starving now. I could murder a pizza. I might ring out for one.' She leant over to her drawer. 'Mum didn't leave any money.' Bianca lay back dejectedly on the pillows.

Children this ill were invariably and understandably spoilt by the staff. If their day could be made easier with a new video game or something nice to eat, the ward funds covered it, and Lucinda had no doubt that this case would be no exception.

'I'm sure we can stretch to a pizza. Do you want me to ask Ann to order you one?'

Bianca shook her head. 'I can ring myself. I've got my own phone,' she said importantly. 'But the nurses are all busy and all the other kids are asleep. I'm the oldest on the ward except for Toby and he's too sick. It's no fun eating pizza on your own.'

Whether it was some sixth sense of Ann's that she heeded or not, for some reason Lucinda didn't ignore Bianca's hidden plea.

'I guess I haven't eaten yet. All right, then, you ring for a pizza and I'll stay for a slice—on one condition, though.'

'Name it,' Bianca wheezed.

'You let me take some blood and have a quick listen to your chest.'

Bianca rang for the food while Lucinda collected the various pieces of equipment she would need to take Bianca's blood. Wheeling the stainless-steel trolley to the bedside, she smiled as Bianca grudgingly offered her arm.

'I'm going to listen to your chest first.'

Bianca sat forward and matter-of-factly lifted her gown. Her chest sounded as bad as ever but not worse, as far as Lucinda could tell.

'I'll do the blood now. What did you order?' she asked by way of distraction as she swabbed the area and slipped the needle in.

'Supreme, but with no anchovies. How much are you taking?' Bianca yelped. 'I'll have none left the way you lot carry on.'

'I haven't finished yet.' Lucinda transferred the blood from the syringe into the various tubes and bottles she had selected. 'I'm going to do some blood gases as well.'

'What tests are you doing?'

'The usual—a full blood examination to check for any anaemia or signs of infection, U and Es to check for any electrolyte imbalance, and also some blood cultures.'

'They normally only take them when I've got a temperature,' Bianca said knowingly.

Lucinda nodded as she took the arterial blood gases from

the young girl's wrist. 'That's right, there's supposed to be more chance of isolating bugs when the temperature's high and the infection is particularly active, but sometimes an infection still shows up when the temperature's normal and you're least expecting it. Now, you press on that for a few minutes while I get rid of these.'

Lucinda popped the blood gases into a bag of ice and wrote the pathology slips in her extravagant scrawl. Having labelled all the bloods, she placed them in the pathology bags and made her way back to Ann's office.

'I've taken some bloods,' she said to Ann. 'They'll need to go straight down as I've taken blood gases.'

'I'll ring for a porter. What do you think?' Ann asked.

Lucinda retrieved the slips from the bags and wrote 'Urgent' on each order. Shaking her head, she looked up at Ann. 'That you're not happy and that's good enough for me. Everything seems all right on examination, but she is a bit pale and she does seem…' Pausing, Lucinda tried to think of the right words 'A bit clingy perhaps. She's apyrexial and she's on just about every antibiotic we've got in the pharmacy. Still, it's worth doing some blood cultures just in case she's brewing something.' Lucinda hesitated a moment. 'Bianca's ordered a pizza. I said I'd stay for a slice,' she said rather too casually as she made her way out of the office.

'As soft as butter,' Ann called after Lucinda. 'As soft as butter.'

Half an hour later Lucinda pulled the curtains and settled into a seat at Bianca's bedside.

Bianca handed her a slice of pizza, her pale face beaming. 'There you go, Miss Chambers.'

Lucinda felt a stab of pity as she watched Bianca swallow a handful of the enzyme capsules cystic fibrosis patients needed to take before eating in order to help their bodies digest food.

'You can call me Lucinda as we're sharing a pizza,' Lucinda said. 'But tomorrow morning its back to Miss Chambers,' she added sternly as Bianca smiled happily, not remotely bothered by her tone.

'You're very pretty,' Bianca said suddenly.

'Thank you.'

'I wish I was pretty.'

'But you are.' Lucinda said truthfully. 'You're gorgeous.'

'I'm too thin and spotty, and these disgusting braces. Yuk.' She made a face.

'I know how you feel, I had braces at your age but they'll come off soon and it will be more than worth it. Being cooped up in here doesn't help, and once you get the transplant you'll fill out and the spots will go before you know it. You really are going to be very beautiful.'

'If I get the chance,' she said poignantly, and she turned her face to the television screen.

Lucinda had finished her slice of pizza but absent-mindedly she picked up another as she became engrossed in the film Bianca had turned on. The speaker lay on Bianca's pillow, forcing Lucinda to strain to catch all of the words, but it didn't mar her enjoyment—after all, it was one of Lucinda's all-time favourites. They watched in amicable silence, until the young boy on the screen movingly asked his widowed father things to remember about his dead mother. Lucinda turned and saw silent tears pouring down Bianca's face.

'Why don't you turn it over?' she suggested.

Bianca shook her head. 'No, I'm enjoying it, believe it or not.' She gave a loud sniff. 'I'm not afraid of dying for myself. It's just Mum and Dad and my brother, Lewis. I

feel so sorry for them. I know how sad they'll be. I just
wonder how they'll manage.'

Lucinda sat very still. There were times in medicine for
platitudes and optimism in the face of the worst odds. But
there was also a time when the possibility of death, however unwelcome, however vehemently opposed, needed to
be faced. Just because they were talking about it, it didn't
mean they were accepting or giving in. Bianca simply
needed to talk.

'They'd be sad, of course,' Lucinda said after a while.
''Devastated, no doubt, but in time things would get better.
They'd have wonderful memories, and go on loving you
and talking about you. They'd be all right. Have you spoken to them about it?'

'I've tried, but they just get so upset. I want to tell them
I'm not scared and how much I love them, but they just
change the subject.'

'It's hard for them, Bianca, but they know how much
you love them. Sometimes that's the one thing that doesn't
need to be said.'

'Am I going to die?' The question, though half-expected,
still tore through Lucinda.

'Bianca, I can't say no. I want to but I can't, the same
way I can't make that sort of guarantee to any of my patients. But I can promise that I'll do my very best to make
sure you don't, and you have to promise to keep fighting.'

'I lie here at night and I wish more than anything for
new lungs and heart, and then I feel awful because it means
I'm wishing someone dead.'

Lucinda shook her head fiercely. 'No, you're not. You're
wishing you could live and that's entirely different. And,
anyway, wishing doesn't make a scrap of difference.
Terrible things happen, accidents happen. You lying here,
wishing for a new heart and lungs, doesn't change fate. It

would happen anyway. You mustn't feel guilty for wishing you were well.'

Bianca coughed. 'Not well exactly. I'd still have CF, but at least I'd have a clean slate to start with. A new set of lungs for this horrid disease to ruin.'

Lucinda gave her a smile. 'Maybe it won't. There's a lot of progress being made with the treatment of CF but you don't need me to tell you that.' She pointed to the pile of books by the bed. 'I'd better watch my back if you decide to take up medicine. It might be me having to call you Miss Moore.'

Lucinda stood up 'Now, I'm off home. You get some sleep after the film finishes.' She made her way to the curtain, but Bianca called her back.

'Lucinda, is there a happy ending?'

'You'll just have to wait and see,' Lucinda said matter-of-factly, but, seeing Bianca lean back on the pillows, her face softened. 'Of course there's a happy ending,' Lucinda said gently, wishing silently that her words didn't just apply to the film.

Popping her head into the office to say goodnight, she saw Ann tapping away on the computer.

'Are you still here?' Lucinda asked.

'I could say the same for you. I'm just looking to see if any of Bianca's bloods are back. Then I've just got to check the drugs and hopefully then I can get home. Here we are,' she added as the results popped up on the screen. Lucinda looked over her shoulder.

'Nothing out of the ordinary yet for Bianca. I'm off, then. Goodnight.'

Tired now, Lucinda took the lift down one floor and made her way to NICU to check on Kimberley, promising herself a lie-in next morning if her pager didn't go off.

The all-too-familiar sound of the overhead display system crackling into action stopped her in her tracks. As a consultant she wasn't on the cardiac arrest or medical emergency teams, but the hospital had an overhead visual display board that gave information as to where any such emergency was located. The protocol was such that all doctors in the vicinity were to proceed to the area to enable a rapid response. Even before the numbers flickered onto the screen Lucinda just knew what to expect. '000 1 PCUG.' Which translated to 'cardiac arrest, 1st floor, Paediatric Cardiac Unit, General Ward.'

The lifts were out of bounds during any hospital emergency, so Lucinda ran to the stairwell beside the lift, taking the stairs two or three at a time. Coming out onto the corridor, she only just avoided colliding with Seb as he burst out of the spare on-call room. One look at his stricken face told her exactly what he was thinking, and she longed to comfort him.

'I just left the ward,' she said somewhat breathlessly as she ran along with him. 'Billy was fine.' But she knew Seb wouldn't be reassured until he saw his son for himself.

Running onto the ward, they found that ordered chaos reigned. Curtains had been pulled around all the children's beds, leaving only Bianca's exposed. The headrest was off and a nurse was inflating Bianca's lungs with an ambu-bag as Ann knelt astride the young girl, massaging her chest. Another nurse was pulling up drugs and a third was attaching electrodes to Bianca's chest.

'What's the story?' Seb said sharply, instantly taking charge as he took over Bianca's airway, suctioning her deftly. 'Stop the compressions,' he ordered as he expertly inserted a tube down her throat and inflated the cuff, thus securing her airway.

'She's in asystole.' Lucinda said as she checked the monitor.

'I checked her and she seemed fine. I went back less than a minute later to say goodnight and found her like this,' said Ann, resuming the cardiac massage. 'Thank God I went back.'

With Seb in control of Bianca's airway, Lucinda was free to concentrate on her heart. 'So she hasn't been down long?' Lucinda said as she inserted various drugs into Bianca's intravenous line. 'Keep up the massage for a minute, Ann—give these drugs a chance to work.' Ann pumped away as the cardiac arrest team arrived, but they didn't take over as the team already working on Bianca was far more senior. Instead, they assisted, all working together to save this precious young life.

'OK, stop,' Lucinda ordered. Every eye was on the monitor. A rhythm was picked up. 'Sinus bradycardia,' Lucinda said. 'Give me some more adrenaline.' A syringe containing the cardiac stimulant was immediately passed to her.

'Adrenaline 1 in 10,000—3 mls,' Lucinda stated as she gave the drug. It was duly charted, along with the time given, by a nurse. Bianca's heart rate picked up. 'Normal sinus rhythm,' Lucinda said with a note of triumph as she looked around the bedside. 'Well done, everyone.'

'She's fighting the tube,' Seb said. 'I'm going to sedate her and we'll get her over to Intensive Care stat. It's all right, little lady.' Seb spoke tenderly into Bianca's ear. 'You're going to be OK now.' The sedative drugs took effect and Seb, Lucinda and the arrest team wheeled Bianca to the PICU as the other staff set about tidying and replacing the equipment on the resuscitation trolley and settling the other children, who had been awoken by the commotion.

The cardiothoracic physician arrived shortly after they got to PICU and Lucinda handed over to him.

'Poor kid,' he said when she'd finished. 'And her poor

parents, too. Ann just rang to say they're on the way. I'm not looking forward to talking to them.'

Seb had walked over to join them and Lucinda suddenly found herself momentarily tongue-tied.

'Not the nicest part of the job, I guess, but someone has to do it,' Lucinda said crisply, and then inwardly kicked herself. It had been an emotional night and in an attempt to maintain her composure she had again come across as clinical and uncaring.

The look that passed between the two men didn't go unnoticed by Lucinda.

'I'm just going to check on Ann,' Seb said, breaking the uncomfortable silence. '*She'll* be pretty upset by what's happened.'

Lucinda heard the inference and in an attempt to redeem herself offered her assistance. 'I'll come along, too.'

Seb merely shrugged and didn't say a word as they walked across to the ward. Only when they got to the doors did he speak. 'Just go easy on her, Lucinda. They're more than just patients to Ann.'

'Fancy another coffee?' Ann offered, her voice heavy.

Lucinda nodded her acceptance and took a seat. Over and over the evening's events Ann went, picking Lucinda's brains, desperately searching for a reason for Bianca's sudden crash, but Lucinda simply couldn't come up with an answer. Finally it was Seb who put the night's events into perspective.

'Who knows why, Ann? It isn't always clear-cut. Maybe the blood cultures will show up a massive infection, maybe it was a mucous plug, perhaps her little body had simply had enough.'

'Maybe she was just unlucky,' Ann said, and Lucinda saw the sparkle of tears in her eyes.

'She was bloody lucky if you ask me,' said Seb in a firm voice.

Lucinda and Ann turned to him questioningly.

'I'd hardly call her lucky.' Ann said sharply.

'Oh, I don't know. If she was going to arrest anyway, what are the chances of having a cardiothoracic and an anaesthetic consultant ten seconds away, along with a charge nurse with a hunch who hovered around all night instead of going home? I tell you this much—if ever my number's up I wouldn't mind having such a crack team in the vicinity.' Ann gave a small smile and Lucinda knew Seb had made her feel better—herself, too, for that matter—but Seb wasn't done cheering Ann up yet.

'You know Ann's nickname, don't you?' he asked Lucinda.

''Don't, Seb,' Ann begged, but he wasn't going to be deflected.

'The Resuscitator!'

Lucinda let out a throaty laugh. 'I've been called worse.'

Ann joined in the laughter, visibly better for the light-hearted banter that might have seemed callous to some, given the previous tragic events, but when you dealt with life-and-death situations regularly black humour was almost mandatory to save you from going under. Ann picked up her bag. 'I'm off. I'd better find out what my feral teenage sons are getting up to without Mum on a balmy Saturday night. If you think Billy's causing you sleepless nights now, Seb, just wait until he hits puberty—the fun really begins then. My boys will turn me grey.'

Ann bustled off.

'She's great, isn't she?' Lucinda stated.

'Golden. I asked her to change her annual leave when Billy's op was brought forward so she'd be on duty while he was a patient, and she did. Nothing against the other staff, of course, but Ann really is one in a million.' He stood up and flicked the venetian blinds. Lucinda watched his strong profile illuminated by the ward lights as he gazed out at his sleeping son, and she felt the familiar knot of tension in her stomach that occurred when Seb was around. 'I feel so guilty,' he said out of the blue.

'Why?' Lucinda demanded.

'All the time I was running to the ward I was just praying that it wasn't Billy.'

'Of course you were. Billy's your son.' Lucinda recalled the conversation she'd so recently had with Bianca and felt her throat tighten. 'Just because you were wishing it wasn't Billy, it doesn't mean you wanted it to be Bianca.'

Seb turned and gave her a thin smile. 'I need some air. One week exclusively breathing the hospital's air-conditioning is sending me crazy. Will you join me?'

They took the lift and then the stairwell up to the roof. The air seemed to hum with tension and Lucinda wondered if she was imagining things. Could this beautiful man possibly be feeling the same way about her? Had he felt that instant attraction, too? Surely not, she reasoned. He had his mind on other things at the moment and evidently he thought she was as hard as nails. But as he took her arm and led her across the roof she was acutely aware of his touch, and Lucinda was positive his hand lingered a moment as they came to stand on the roof's edge.

Her legs felt somewhat unsteady, and it had nothing to do with vertigo, Lucinda acknowledged as she leant against the wall and looked out over the City. The view was almost identical to the one from her apartment. Flinders Street Station was lit up like a fairground, the arts centre like a miniature Eiffel Tower. It was stunning and so much better shared.

'Times like this I almost wish I smoked.' Seb said, his voice carrying in the night air.

'No, you don't.'

For an age Seb stood quite still, drinking in the view. Finally he spoke. 'Billy will be home next week, and the week after that I'm expected back at work.'

'You and Gemma will manage,' she said with more conviction than she felt.

He turned and faced her then and Lucinda saw the pain in his features.

'Gemma's leaving to live in New South Wales, a job offer she "simply couldn't refuse" came up.'

Lucinda gasped. 'Does Billy know?'

'Yep, we've known for a couple of weeks. It hit him pretty hard. She'd made her mind up before we knew that Billy's operation was going to be moved forward. It's all too far gone for her to put it off and, anyway, I think that now Billy knows it's going to happen it might just be better to get it over and done with so we can all start to move on. It's been pretty tough for a while on all of us.'

'Seb, that's awful. I don't know what to say,' she said truthfully.

'Not so awful. I got Billy out of it. I'd go through the whole thing ten times over for that—all I want is for Billy to be happy.'

'But how will you cope?' She voiced his fears for him.

'I don't know,' he said heavily. 'I just don't know. Since we divorced, Gemma's hardly been around but any help is better than none. My sister Isabella is coming down for a month when I have to go back to work, and she's bringing her kids. She lives in Ballarat, though. I can't keep relying on her—she's got a life, too. I'm going to have to do a lot of thinking. There's going to have to be some changes. Anyway,' he said, 'that's enough about me. What about you, Miss Chambers? You look like a woman who knows where she's heading. So what's it to be—professor, chief of staff? What is it you want out of life?'

Lucinda hesitated. Seb had been so open, so honest that she wanted to tell him her dream, but how could she when it was something she hardly dared admit even to herself? How could she tell him that a part-time GP juggling too many children's packed lunches sounded good from here? He would never understand. 'We'll see,' Lucinda said non-committally. 'Consultant will do for now.' She shivered suddenly. 'It's windy up here. I'm cold.'

'That can be fixed.' Seb's voice was deep and she was sure she could hear an invitation in his words, but Lucinda wavered, filled with uncertainty. The temptation to slip into his arms, to be warmed and comforted, was overwhelming; but what if she was wrong? What if she had misread the signs? If he moved just an inch, gave some further indication as to what he was implying, she would have gone to him without hesitation. But instead she stood there, staring at him for the longest time, until it was Seb who dragged his eyes away.

'We'd better go back down' he said eventually. 'Billy might wake up.'

Lucinda managed a smile. 'You go,' she said quietly. 'I might stay up here a while, take in the view.'

'Later,' he murmured, and then he was gone.

Lucinda hugged her arms to her chest, colder now without him near. Careful, she warned herself, tread carefully. Sebastian Carlisle would be very easy to fall in love with but he came as a package—Seb and Billy. It was a serious consideration, one that could only lead to complications, and Billy was simply too precious to even consider hurting.

CHAPTER FOUR

CONCENTRATING on her stroke as she cut through the empty pool, Lucinda found a temporary escape from the jumbled emotions that had kept her awake for most of the night. After ten laps she climbed out of the water, making her way to the poolside shower. The icy cold jets were refreshing and invigorating. For a moment she contemplated using the gym equipment—after all, the endless take-aways had to catch up sooner or later. Instead she dried herself and dressed casually in khaki shorts and a linen blouse, tying her damp hair back with a scrunchie.

Southbank was setting up for the day, and a few revellers were stretching out Saturday night, buoyed up by their casino winnings, and were singing as they walked along the riverside. Lucinda bought the Sunday papers and settled herself at a cane table shielded from the early morning sun by a large umbrella. She ordered a café latte and as she had done ten lengths of the pool succumbed to the waiter's suggestion of warm croissants with butter and honey.

Melbourne was awakening. Joggers and power-walkers strutted their stuff along the riverbank, effortlessly avoiding the pavement artists who were touching up their work. The huge turrets that flanked the casino were shooting flames half-hourly in an impressive performance that seemed to go unnoticed by the regulars, but to the uninitiated like Lucinda it was breathtaking. Bianca would love it here.

In that instant Lucinda acknowledged the real reason for her insomnia. The time she had spent with Seb last night had been pleasantly unsettling to say the least, but it hadn't kept her awake. If anything, she had longed to go to sleep just to relive those moments again. No, the real reason she had tossed and turned had been a little girl who had been given only the smallest shot at life. Lucinda felt the sting of tears in her eyes and grappled in her bag for her sunglasses. Why couldn't they just stay nameless? Instead, it was Bianca, Billy, Kimberley and countless other children who had come before them. She remembered the name of every child that had died in her care, and it hurt. It really hurt. Reaching for her mobile, she started to dial the hospital's number then decided against it. Bianca deserved a bit more than a phone call so instead Lucinda settled her bill and made her way across the bridge to the hospital.

Instead of going straight to Paediatric Intensive Care she made her way to the cardiac ward, with the excuse that she was checking on all her patients. But deep down the thought of entering PICU and not seeing Bianca there was too upsetting. The news, if bad, would be gentler coming from Ann.

She didn't need an excuse. Ann knew why she was there as soon as she saw her.

'Couldn't sleep, huh?'

'How is she?'

Ann gave a small shrug. 'Still alive, but only just. She had a massive MI in the early hours. Thirteen years old and she's had a heart attack.'

'Why wasn't I called? She could have—'

Ann shook her head. 'They're treating her conservatively or you'd have been paged long ago. She's not a candidate for surgery—she just wouldn't survive. What she needs is a transplant. She's been moved to the top of the list, so maybe a match will come in soon. Don't go too far this weekend—hopefully we'll be needing you. You've got your pager?'

Lucinda lifted her blouse slightly and showed the pager, used only for transplants, strapped firmly to her belt. 'Glued to me. I'd better go over to PICU and have a look at her.'

Ann nodded. 'Her parents want to talk to you.'

'To me? Do they want to go through the transplant procedure?'

Ann shook her head. 'No, it's a bit more personal than that. I told them how you'd watched a film with her last night. I guess they just need to hear how she was.'

'I'm not exactly dressed properly,' Lucinda said somewhat formally, in a vain attempt to delay the inevitable.

'I'm sure that's the least of their concerns,' Ann said. 'It would mean a lot to them if you had a quick word.'

Lucinda nodded her assent, and turned to go.

As she made her way out of the ward an angry little bundle dressed in pyjamas and a dressing-gown rushed past her, just about sending her flying.

'Whoa, there.' She grabbed hold of the dressing-gown and turned the little boy around.

'Where are you off to in such a hurry, Billy? You shouldn't be running on the ward, you know.'

He gave her an indignant look.

'I was going to the toilet, but there isn't any paper,' he said accusingly, as if it was her fault.

'Well, I'm sure the cleaners will be here soon, or the nurses will be out on handover in a while.'

'But I need to go *now*,' he said simply.

Lucinda looked around. Not a domestic in sight, and the only nurse left on the ward was giving some intravenous drugs to a patient. Lucinda picked up a box of tissues from the nurses' station. 'Here,' she said. 'Use these.'

Billy looked at her as if she'd gone completely mad.

'I can't use these. Ann said we weren't to waste tissues.'

'I think she was referring to the paper aeroplanes you

were all making with them the other day. I'm sure she won't mind.'

But Billy wasn't going to be deflected.

'I need some toilet paper.'

His little face worked up as if he might start crying and Lucinda sensed the urgency in his demand.

'OK,' she said with a sigh. 'You go on to the toilet and I'll bring you some.'

'You won't forget?'

'Cross my heart.' He hurried off and Lucinda spent the next five minutes trying to locate the store cupboard. Finally she found it and, rummaging around, she gave a little laugh. This was ridiculous. She was a consultant, taking orders from a five-year-old. Still, when you had to go...

Finally she found the paper and made her way back to the toilets in time to find Billy at the sink, washing his hands.

'Here you are.'

'I found some,' he said. 'On the window-ledge. But thanks.' He took the roll and placed it under his dressing-gown.

'What are you doing?'

'I'm going to keep it in my locker—they're always running out here.' He turned and stared directly at Lucinda. 'Is Bianca dead?' he asked completely out of the blue.

Lucinda hesitated, somewhat taken back by the direct-ness of his question. 'No, she's been moved to the intensive care ward.'

'That's what Ann said, but I thought she was just trying not to upset me. Is it her heart?'

Lucinda nodded. 'Sort of.'

'Well, if it's her heart, why can't you fix it? You fixed mine.'

'It's a bit more complicated than that, but I am going to

try. I'm going to talk to her parents now.' Billy finished drying his hands.

'Bye, then.' He gave her the benefit of his cheeky grin and ambled back to his bed, carefully depositing the precious paper in his locker first.

Lucinda shook her head and smiled. Really, he was just too cute.

She put on a theatre gown and washed her hands before she entered the PICU. The next half-hour was spent with the registrar, going over Bianca's results. From the workstation she could see Bianca, her thin body covered by a sheet, attached to the monitors she so fiercely hated. Her terrified parents and brother were sitting rigid at her side, willing her to hold on, to fight to stay alive. It was indeed a heartbreaking scene but Lucinda pushed aside all emotion and concentrated on the task in hand. Bianca needed her medical skills, no more, or so she thought. When her discussion with the registrar concluded and they both resignedly agreed that all they could do was continue the current treatment and wait for Bianca's ship to come in, she asked the charge nurse to bring Bianca's parents to the interview room. Outside the door Lucinda took a few deep breaths before she knocked and entered. The sorrow in the faces that greeted her was familiar.

'Mr and Mrs Moore, I'm Miss Chambers. You asked to speak with me?'

'Oh, Doctor, thank you for coming in to see Bianca this morning.'

Lucinda gave a small nod. 'I've been talking with Mr Hill, the PICU registrar, and for now all we can do is wait and hope for a suitable donor.'

'Sister Benton said you spent some time with Bianca last night before she...' Mrs Moore struggled to speak. 'Before she was taken so ill. We wanted to thank you. It would

have meant so much to Bianca. She thinks a lot of you—
you're her favourite.'

'Me?' Lucinda said surprised. 'But I've only been in the
hospital a week. Surely she would have had others…'

Mrs Moore gave a small laugh through her tears. 'You
know what teenagers are like. Bianca thought you were so
"cool". She was raving on and on about you. When Sister
Benton called and broke the news she said that you'd
shared a pizza and watched a film with her. It probably
didn't mean much to you—I understand that—but for
Bianca, well, she doesn't have much of a life. Last night
would have been very special to her. She really admires
you.'

Lucinda's eyes misted over and she hastily looked down
at the notes in front of her. It was a trick she often used.
The writing might as well have been in Chinese but it gave
her something to do, something other than looking into Mr
and Mrs Moore's tortured eyes. After a moment she looked
up at the strained faces, desperate to hear something—anything—about their daughter.

She faltered for a moment unsure of how much of their
conversation to reveal, unsure if she could do this and still
remain in control, but deep down she knew Bianca's words
weren't hers to keep. They had been meant for Bianca's
family.

'Bianca spoke about you all last night.' She smiled
gently at Lewis, a ten-year-old who should have been out
at the beach or on his skateboard, not sitting in an intensive
care interview room, trying to comfort his parents. 'How
much she loved you, how much you loved her. Bianca also
told me that she wasn't scared of dying. Her main concern
was how you'd all cope if it happened.'

The sob that escaped from Mr Moore's lips tore through
Lucinda. Instinctively he reached for his wife and son,

wrapping his arms around them as they sobbed together. Lucinda sat quietly for a couple of moments until they were ready to continue.

'What did you say when Bianca said that?' Mr Moore asked, choking on his tears.

'That you'd be all right, you'd lean on each other and go on loving her wherever she was, and in time the hurt would ease and you'd be left with wonderful memories. I also told her that we had no intention of letting her die, though, and that she had to go on fighting, which she is.'

'Thank you.' He could barely get the words out and Lucinda knew it was time to leave them, to let them comfort each other. 'If you want to talk again just have the PICU staff page me.'

As she made her way along the highly polished corridor, her trainers barely making a sound, Lucinda knew she had done the right thing. Despite the Moores' tears, she had brought comfort to that family, and letting her guard down last night had meant she had got closer to Bianca. Yet surprisingly it hadn't made today any worse. It had actually made it a bit more bearable.

'Sorry, I wasn't looking where I was going.'

'Me neither.' Janine Stewart's red-rimmed eyes met hers as Lucinda bumped into her.

'How's Kimberley?'

'Stable, whatever that means. It's the only word we want to hear at the moment. Whoever said that having a premature baby was like riding on a roller-coaster wasn't wrong.'

'It must be very difficult,' she agreed, knowing how futile her words sounded.

Janine didn't seem to mind. She ran a hand through her untidy hair. 'I'd like to think that this time next year I'll be up to my elbows in nappies and Vegemite toast soldiers, but the dream's starting to fade a bit.'

Lucinda simply didn't know what to say. For the millionth time she berated herself for her inability to vocalise her feelings. The bleeping of her pager came almost as a relief. 'Sorry,' she said apologetically. 'I'll see you on the unit later when I come to check on Kimberley.'

Walking into the canteen, Lucinda picked up the phone to dial the switchboard. Through the glass window she could see Janine slowly making her way back along the corridor, back to her cotside vigil, and not for the first time Lucinda wished she could have said something to help.

The page turned out to be Switchboard merely doing a routine check. Replacing the receiver, she turned and saw Seb eyeing the lunchtime blackboard without much enthusiasm.

Casually she made her way over to him. 'Anything catch your eye?'

He turned and smiled. 'Now it does. You're far more tempting than anything in here.'

Lucinda gave a low laugh. 'I don't think I should let that go to my head. Beef stew and soggy cauliflower are hardly much competition.'

'On the contrary, I happen to be a big fan of the beef stew, and soggy cauliflower is a particular favourite of mine, but I'm thinking of having a splurge and ringing out for dinner tonight.' He paused for a moment. 'Do you fancy sharing a curry with me? We could use the on-call room.'

Lucinda was caught completely off guard. Desperate to accept, but not wanting to appear to eager, she forced herself to pause for a moment before answering. 'That would be great,' she answered casually. 'I'm actually going to be in my office tonight, doing some paperwork.'

Seb smiled. 'I've an even better idea, then. Why don't I

get it sent up to your office if you're going to be in there anyway? At least we'll have some privacy.'

'Sure,' she replied as nonchalantly as she could with her heart in her mouth.

'Great.' He gave her the benefit of his smile. 'I'll look forward to some real food and adult conversation tonight. Billy's hunger for *Robot Savers* hasn't diminished one iota and the rest of the children have got me changing videos, fetching drinks, playing board games and cutting out shapes. It's exhausting. I'll be glad to come back to work for a rest. About eight, then,' he added as he started to go, then changed his mind. 'There is one condition, though,'

Lucinda gave him a quizzical look. 'And what's that?'

'That we talk about you for once. Even I'm getting sick of hearing about me.'

As Lucinda made her way up to NICU her heart was hammering wildly and she scolded herself for overreacting. He had only asked her to share a curry after all; it was no big deal. Pushing the button for the lift, she finally gave in. Who was she kidding? It *was* a huge deal—a night on her own with Sebastian Carlisle!

'How's Kimberley Stewart? Did Andrew review her digoxin levels?' asked Lucinda a little later.

Sue pulled out Kimberley's file—it was twice the weight of the baby.

'Yes, she's in sinus rhythm at the moment. He's going to review her again this afternoon if everything remains stable. Did you want to examine her yourself?'

Lucinda shook her head and Sue gave a relieved smile. 'Good.' Minimal handling was the order of the day for babies as sick as this and Lucinda wasn't going to do anything to upset the apple cart.

'Where's Janine?' Lucinda asked. 'She started to talk to

me in the canteen but my pager went off. She seemed upset.'

'She is. Mark goes back to work tomorrow—she's helping him pack now. Mark's upset because he feels that he's abandoning them and Janine's upset because she feels he's deserting them. It's like a tragic soap story. If only they'd sit down and talk they'd probably get somewhere.'

An idea was forming in Lucinda's mind and she surprised even herself as the white lie slipped easily from the mouth. 'I won a dinner for two at Surayan's Indian Restaurant, but it has to be used by this weekend. I'm on call, so that rules me out and, anyway, I've got plans. Perhaps you could persuade Janine and Mark to use it. After all, the distance to the restaurant isn't much further than the canteen. You can always ring them if there's any change.'

'That's really nice of you.' Sue gave her a quizzical look. 'Are you sure you don't mind? If I could persuade them to go, it could do a lot of good. I'd already suggested they go out tonight for their anniversary but money's very tight for them at the moment.'

Lucinda shrugged dismissively. 'It's no big deal. See what they say. I'll put a booking in their name for about eight. It's up to them whether they use it or not. You can only take the horse to water after all.'

After ringing Surayan's and letting Vijay in on the charade, Lucinda took the chance to do some sightseeing. As she was on call she couldn't roam too far, but St Kilda beach was only a short tram ride away and if needed she could hail a taxi and be back at the hospital within minutes. It was totally unlike her more junior days where being on call had meant you had to stay in the hospital at all times so as to be immediately available for any emergency. Now it was the more junior doctors' turns and she would be called in only for emergency consults or operations.

It still didn't sit quite right with her, though, and invariably Lucinda never strayed too far and liked to pop in and out of the hospital, sometimes choosing to sleep there if worried about a particular patient.

She had been told about the street market St Kilda held on a Sunday and it was as enchanting as promised. Rows and rows of stalls lined the street the length of the beach. Wares were beautifully displayed, all hand-made originals in keeping with a by-law of the market. It was just the place to find a couple of one-offs to add some warmth to her apartment. The only problem was how to get things home, and Lucinda made a mental note to come better prepared next week. Wandering slowly from stall to stall, she settled on a couple of bright throw rugs and some hand-painted prints of the bay.

'I want an ice cream. I want an ice cream.' The piercing shrieks of a young child rose above the crowd. Lucinda turned and watched as two frazzled-looking parents made their way to the ice-cream vendor. 'Not that one.' Red in the face, the little boy flung the cone down onto the pavement and proceeded to cry loudly. His exasperated parents reluctantly bought another cone in a bid to quieten him.

What a terror, Lucinda thought to herself. Again she questioned the rationale behind pursuing a relationship with Seb. Her time off was precious enough without spending it with a child battling with her for his father's attention. There you go again, she thought, checking herself. You're only sharing a curry, not the rest of your lives. And anyway, she consoled herself, Billy was far too laid-back to throw a temper tantrum over an ice-cream cone—he only seemed to get upset about toilet rolls. A small chuckle escaped from her lips at the memory and Lucinda realised she was actually walking along, smiling just at the thought of him. What was it with Seb and Billy Carlisle? she wondered. And what on earth was happening to her?

Happy with her purchases, she started to make her way back to the tram stop, but a particular stall she had missed earlier caught her eye. Soft organza dresses hanging from the canopy fluttered gently in the breeze in a myriad shades from the palest lemon to a vibrant purple. They had all been tie-dyed. The colours gently ran into each other, adding a depth to the simply cut dresses.

They were completely different to anything she usually wore, but Lucinda was hooked and more so when she saw the price—about a tenth of what she usually paid for a dress, which made an impulse buy all the more irresistible. Settling on a pale lilac, she finally clambered onto the tram, her purchases taking up two seats, and settled back for the short journey home.

Her busy week, combined with the previous night's insomnia, made her unmade bed all too appealing. It was easier to climb in and rest awhile than bother making it. For once sleep came easily, and by the time Lucinda awoke it was well after seven. Cursing herself for not setting the alarm, she showered quickly and, pulling her new dress from the bag, slipped it on. It was stunning, gently ruched around the bust, its flowing length doing nothing to hide her curves and the lilac bringing colour to her face. She left her hair down and tied on some canvas espadrilles. A final glance in the mirror and she was ready.

The curry was delivered to her office promptly at eight and Lucinda set up the room for the meal. Candles would have been way over the top, of course, but her desk lamp provided a warm glow. Hastily she opened a file and started to write—she was supposed to be doing some paperwork after all. Just as she was starting to get nervous, wondering if it was actually going to be Seb that didn't turn up, he knocked on the door. Looking up from her desk, she tried to casually smile as her heart somersaulted. Even with his jeans and T-shirt crumpled from lying on Billy's bed, his sex appeal was overwhelming. His hair was as dishevelled as his clothes and she yearned to run her fingers through the wild raven locks.

'Sorry I'm late. Billy took a while to settle and, of course, I ended up dozing off. They've started playing this New-Age rainforest music at the children's settling time. Doesn't work a scrap on the children but it knocks me out like a light.'

Lucinda laughed at his explanation. 'I'll have to try it.' Her expression changed 'How is he?' she asked.

'Upset. It's starting to sink in that Gemma's going to Sydney. It's tough on the little guy.'

'And you, too?' she ventured.

But Seb wasn't going to be drawn. 'Oh, I'm all right—just starving. That curry smells marvellous.'

Lucinda smiled and closed the file she'd been pretending to read. 'Let's eat, then.'

'What work are you doing?' he asked as she spooned the rice onto the plates.

'Just compiling some research I was doing in Queensland. The paperwork it produces is horrific.'

'Tell me about it. I just finished a trial on PCA in paediatrics,' Seb said, referring to patient-controlled analgesia, a means of giving pain relief in an infusion which was controlled by the patient. A touch of a button meant the patient could administer more pain relief if desired. It was strictly controlled with a lock-out mechanism so patients couldn't overdose. Widely used with adults, it was becoming more common for some paediatric patients, and the trials were promising.

'I'm supposed to be presenting my findings next month at the medical conference in Queensland, though I'll struggle to have it all completed. Are you going?' he asked as they settled down to eat.

'Professor Hays did mention it. He said he had a wedding to attend but I rather think he's had enough of medical conferences. I'll probably be there but only for a couple of days over the weekend. We've got a lot of theatre cases the following week. It will be busy from then right up until Christmas.'

Seb nodded. 'The bulk of the conference is over the weekend anyway. The other days are more of an opportunity for a bit of a holiday. I'm only staying two nights as well. Gemma's going to be in Melbourne to see Billy as it will be too soon for him to fly to Sydney. Anyway, I've promised to cover for another consultant—Chris King—on the Sunday afternoon so he can go to a wedding, probably the same one as the prof. I owe a lot of favours,' he added. 'Now Billy's op is out of the way it's time to pay a few back.'

'I'm sure people don't want to be paid back. They understand how hard it is for you.'

'I doubt it,' he said. 'Anyway, I came here on the understanding we talked about you. So, tell me, what's it like, being the daughter of two famous cosmetic surgeons?'

'It's different,' Lucinda said cagily.

'And did your stunning looks come courtesy of your parents' genes or their scalpels?'

Lucinda laughed. 'A bit of both actually. Mum and Dad mostly, but nothing would stop my mother in the quest for a perfect daughter. I thank the heavens daily that I was born reasonably OK or I'd have been nipped, tucked and re-shaped beyond recognition by now.'

'You're not serious?' Seb said incredulously.

Lucinda pulled back her hair. 'I had my ears pulled back when I was nine. I've seen old photos and they hardly stuck out at all.' She paused. 'Well, not that much. I had to wear this awful turban-like bandage for a week afterwards. I've had braces put on perfectly good teeth just so I could have a cover-girl smile, and my adolescent pimples were treated by a hysterical mother sending me off to dermatologists for antibiotics and creams.'

'Good heavens.'

'Fortunately I spent most of my teenage years at boarding school so most of the lumps and bumps and ugly stages all teenagers go through happened well out of the way of my parents or you could be sitting opposite quite a different-looking woman now.'

'How was it—boarding school?'

'I didn't mind it too much,' she hedged. 'What are your parents like?'

'Actually, they're both dead.'

'I'm sorry.'

'Don't be. I had a fabulous childhood. I'd love them to still be here, of course, but I know how lucky I've been when I hear stories like yours. I just can't imagine what it would have been like going to bed without giving your mum a kiss and Sunday dinners and all that sort of thing.'

'Well, there's the difference. I never had any of that, even when I was home on holidays. You can't miss what you don't know.'

'Oh, yes, you can.' He looked at her then, right into her eyes. Lucinda swallowed hard. He was right. She had missed so many things—the Sunday roasts, the unconditional love of a parent. With her parents it had all been about achieving. And now she missed intimacy even though she had never really known it.

'I worry that's what will happen to Billy. I can't keep

relying on my sister and nannies—he needs some stability. Boarding school might have to be an option.'

No, she wanted to shout. The idea of little Billy at boarding school was too awful to comprehend. He'd seen enough of institutions to last him a lifetime, she thought, but it wasn't her place to add to Seb's fears.

'I survived,' she said instead, her heart filled with an overwhelming sadness. No mum or dad to ask him how his day was at the dinner table or tuck him in at night. Limits on *Robot Savers*. That beautiful personality quietly stifled. Despite what she had said to Seb, though she had thought it all right at the time, with the benefit of hindsight it had been awful. It was there that she had learnt to hide her feelings, waving Mum and Dad off at the start of term. Kids needed their parents. She knew that now and was painfully aware of what she had missed out on.

The conversation flowed easily, and although they were only drinking diet cola Lucinda found herself telling Seb things she hadn't even thought about in years, letting him in on a side of herself she rarely if ever revealed. He was an amazingly good listener, and by the time the curry had been eaten and the remnants packed away there was only one thing they hadn't yet shared. Seb seemed to read her mind as the night came to a conclusion. For a moment the room was quiet, except for the hum of sexual tension, and then he gave her a small smile.

'You look beautiful tonight. I like you in that dress. It's very feminine, not that you need any help with that.

'I'm not all power suits and fitted dresses,' she lied, thinking this was the one garment she possessed that wasn't fully lined and dry-clean only.

Slowly, purposefully, Seb walked around the desk. Taking Lucinda's hands as she stood up, he pulled her towards him.

Lucinda was tall and in her espadrilles, despite Seb's height, her eyes were nearly level with his. He hardly had to bend his head to kiss her and their lips found each other easily. His hands, warm through the flimsy material, pulled her closer yet and she melted into his embrace. He was truly wonderful to kiss and Lucinda lost herself in the moment until he gently pulled away.

'I'd better go. It would be very easy to go and do something really silly here.'

Lucinda gave a little grumble and laid her head on his chest. He was right. She knew they shouldn't make love, not here and not so soon, but her resistance around this man was practically zero.

'Like what?' she said huskily, not wanting the evening to end, but his answer to her seductive question came as such a surprise that for once she was completely lost for words.

'Like fall in love.' He gently kissed the top of her head. 'I'd better get back.'

Dumbly she nodded, and stood quite still as he left. He felt it, too, it wasn't just her! How on earth she wondered, was she supposed to sleep after that?

CHAPTER FIVE

DESPITE the success of his surgery, Billy wasn't ready to go home by Monday. His asthma was still proving difficult to control and at the ward round it was decided to keep him in for a few more days to change his medication and continue with the aggressive physiotherapy. So far he hadn't developed a chest infection, but all the ingredients were there for one to manifest and it was safer to keep him in.

Seb's only concern was for his son and he ruffled his grumbling son's hair. Gemma, however, looked far from pleased by the news, but the round moved on before she had a chance to voice her objections. The rest of the round went fairly smoothly until they arrived at Bianca's bedside on PICU. Lucinda had to bite her tongue as Pete Hughes described his version of Saturday night's events.

'I popped into the ward in the evening to review the patients and Sister Benton seemed somewhat concerned about young Bianca. I reviewed her thoroughly but I couldn't find anything wrong. She seemed fine.'

'Very good.' Professor Hays nodded as he peered through the thick file that contained Bianca's notes. 'A lot of blood tests were done—excellent.' He carried on reading. 'I see you reviewed her as well, Miss Chambers?'

Lucinda gave a short nod, inwardly seething. Pete had let the professor assume it had been him that had taken Bianca's blood when in truth he hadn't even bothered to go anywhere near the patient. But to say anything here would be wrong. She would deal with Pete privately.

70

'That's right. I couldn't find anything significant either. She arrested just after I left.'

'Well, let's hope a donor becomes available soon for Bianca, though realistically I think we're getting past the hoping stage with Bianca. She really isn't a suitable candidate and the heart and lungs might be better suited to someone with a more realistic chance of survival.'

'No.' The words escaped from Lucinda's lips before she even realised she had spoken. Everyone turned and stared, surprised by her passionate outburst. But Lucinda knew that for Bianca her eleventh hour had come. She was fading fast and her life was governed now by the machines she so hated. Paralysed and sedated by drugs she had no chance to fight now, it was up to Lucinda to do it for her.

She recovered her composure quickly. 'I actually think Bianca will do very well, given the chance. Her strength is amazing—that's the only reason she's survived as long as she has and the reason that, despite the rapid progression of her disease, she was still deemed "too well" to be at the top of the list for a transplant.' Lucinda went on, her outburst quickly forgotten as she argued Bianca's case in an almost detached manner, relaying medical and technical details with such an air of authority that she knew as she concluded her persuasive speech she had won the argument—for now.

'Well, let's hope something comes up soon,' Professor Hays said, and Lucinda breathed an inward sigh of relief. He turned to Pete Hughes. 'Excellent work. It's good to be seen at the weekends. Patients are still sick. Perhaps you'd like to operate tomorrow, we've got a couple of interesting cases. Maybe it's time to see how much I've taught you. Miss Chambers and I will assist, of course.' Professor Hays marched off to his office as the entourage dispersed.

'Just a moment, Pete,' Lucinda called as he made his

way down the corridor. 'If I might have a brief word.' Pete gave a small nod and walked towards her, meeting her head on. She saw that his surly face had a look of defiance. 'In my office.'

She closed the door but didn't sit down. Dispensing with any niceties, she cut straight to the chase.

'You just popped in to check on the patients? You reviewed Bianca thoroughly? Are we talking about the same night here? How about you were hanging around the ward waiting to pick up your latest girlfriend and you had a cursory glance at her notes? That would be somewhat nearer the mark.'

'I had more than a "cursory glance" and Bianca was dozing. I thought it better to let her rest.'

'Oh, come on, Pete, that's no excuse and you damn well know it,' Lucinda snapped, furious at his indifference.

'You said yourself there was nothing abnormal to find. You're the great consultant. What makes you think that I, a mere registrar, would have found anything different? Why do you think that I might pick up something you missed?' So Seb had been right, that *was* what his problem was. Well, it was time to deal with it.

'Oh, that's the last thing I'm thinking, I can assure you of that. We both know you think this should be your office, that you should have got the job, but at the end of the day you didn't, and in my opinion the best doctor won. If it's a consultant's position you're after, Pete, you'd better start lifting your game. Next time a nurse is concerned, particularly one as senior as Ann Benton, try looking at the patient, not the notes.'

'Have you finished?' He spat the words through gritted teeth.

'For now.' She stood back as he brushed past and marched out of the office. Sitting at her desk, she put her head in her hands and took a deep breath. Lucinda had taken no pleasure in the confrontation, but Pete had to be brought in to line. She needed him and relied on him too much for him to be slacking off. If he missed something, then potentially so did she. But there wasn't time to dwell on her argument with Pete, for just as a watched kettle never boiled, the one time since Saturday night that she hadn't been consciously wishing it would go off, the shrill bleeps of her transplant pager broke the silence. Grabbing the phone, she dialled the numbers. Please, let it be for Bianca, please, let it be for Bianca, she prayed silently as she calmly went through the motions. Someone must have been listening. Bianca's ship had just come in—a near-perfect match!

All animosity with Pete was put firmly aside as the transplant team swung into action. More blood was taken from Bianca and the final checks were made that would determine if she was going to receive this precious chance. Flight teams were despatched to retrieve the organs, and in the hospital everyone came together. Each played their essential part, working alongside each other, from the professor down to the domestic staff who would prepare her post-operative room in the intensive care ward, meticulously cleaning and sterilising it to ensure the chance of post-operative infection was minimised. Each had a vital role to play and all did their best.

But finally when the arduous operation was completed it was left up to Bianca. The perfusionist weaned her off by-pass and all held their breath as the new heart and lungs perfused. No matter how many times this operation had been performed, for all the staff watching it was still like seeing a miracle take place. Before she had even left the theatre Bianca's colour was better than it had been in ages. Her oxygen readings reached new highs.

But her little body's reserves were woefully depleted. The last few days had taken their toll on her already fragile health and there wasn't much left to guard her for the long battle that lay ahead. Finally she was wheeled back to the huge sterile room in the intensive care unit, through the heavy double doors that would hopefully help to keep out infection which, along with rejection, was her biggest enemy.

Lucinda spoke with Bianca's parents, but she was guarded with her optimism. Bianca had been given a chance but there was still a very long way to go. And then it was back to Bianca's bedside where she spent the next few hours working alongside the anaesthetist and the nursing staff in the impossibly warm room, made worse by the gown, hat and mask she had to wear. Only when she was sure Bianca was stable did she leave her side and make her way to the on-call coffee-room.

Exhausted, she leant back on the sofa and closed her eyes for a moment, glad of the peace without the constant bleeping of monitors and hiss of the respirator, glad to be alone. But when she opened them, Seb was standing there like a beautiful mirage and Lucinda realised that she didn't really want to be alone, and Seb was the one person she wanted to see.

He understood how fatigued she was, that the day had taken its toll.

'You did a great job. I came and watched for a while from the viewing gallery.'

She gave a half-smile.

'I wish it had been a few days ago. Bianca would have been so much stronger then.'

'I know, but there's more takers than givers—we can only do our best with what's available. She's got a chance now.'

Lucinda didn't reply, she knew what he was saying was right. Bianca had received a precious gift, but in a perfect world she wouldn't have had to wait so long. But then again, she reflected, in a perfect world she wouldn't have been born with CF and the donor's family wouldn't be crying tonight, too, in agony over the death of a loved one. Lucinda's heart went out to these unknown people, who in the depths of despair had made the bravest and most generous of decisions, who had somehow managed to rise above their grief for a moment and give hope to another family.

'What are you thinking?' His words gently broke into her thoughts.

Normally she would have stiffened and given some vague reply about her workload or charts that need to be written, but under Seb's gaze she could only be honest. 'About the donor's family.'

Seb didn't say anything, he just walked quietly over to the coffee percolator and poured her a cup.

'How's Billy?'

'Good, thoroughly spoilt. I'll need a second mortgage to pay for all the Robot videos he's demanding.'

'How are you?'

He shrugged, his hand pausing a moment too long as he went to pour the milk. 'Getting there. Gemma went to Sydney this afternoon.'

'I thought she wasn't due to go for another week or so.'

Seb nodded. 'You know how much she hates the hospital. She's gone to get the move started and then she'll fly back once Billy's discharged. She's going to spend a couple of weeks with him once he's out of hospital. It works out better actually. Isabella will still come for a month but not so soon, so I don't have to worry for six weeks yet about babysitters. Still, it was hard for him, saying goodbye.'

And you? she wanted to ask. How did you take her going? There were so many questions buzzing in her head.
Why had they broken up? Why did he have custody? And,
most importantly, did he still have any feelings for
Gemma? But instead of asking, she just sat there quietly,
not wanting to intrude, not wanting to make things worse
for him.

Seb looked at her melancholy face. 'What you need is
chocolate.' He opened one of the on-call rooms and
Lucinda followed him. 'I've got a stash here, Billy gets
heaps and I've had to ration it.' Lucinda sat on the bed as
he broke a bar in two and gave her half. In itself it was no
big deal that she was in there with him. Doctors spent so
much time together it was more like a firemen's dorm than
a bedroom. No one would bat an eye if they walked in now
and saw Lucinda perched on the bed. After all, the door
was open and they were both fully dressed. But for Lucinda
it was a huge deal. She had never been particularly chatty
or friendly with any of her colleagues, not like this anyway.
Her on-call nights in the mess had mainly been spent with
her head in a book, studying for the next lot of exams.

'You're right—I did need chocolate.' She yawned suddenly. 'I had a bit of a confrontation with Pete Hughes this
morning. It got pretty nasty.'

'I'm sure he deserved it. Pete needs bringing into line.'

'Still, it wasn't very pleasant.'

'Look, I know you adore the prof, but I'm sure you'd
have to agree he's not hot on confronting people. He's too
wrapped up in his medicine to deal with the frivolities of
social interaction.'

Lucinda had to reluctantly agree. Professor Hays was
easily the most skilled surgeon she had ever seen, but it
was becoming all too apparent he wasn't a 'people person'.
She thought back to the time he had avoided talking with

Seb and Gemma, how he had given Seb a blow-by-blow account of the surgery he had performed on his son without softening the details.

'Maybe it's a trait amongst cardiothoracic surgeons,' Lucinda said thoughtfully.

Seb looked at her, bemused. 'What on earth are you talking about?'

'Well, let's face it. With the best will in the world you could hardly call me a great communicator. Every time I try to show a bit of compassion I end up sounding like my mother—and if you'd met her you'd realise I wasn't paying myself a compliment. She's the most shallow person you're ever likely to meet.'

'But you're nothing like that,' he argued.

'It's how I come across—you've heard me.'

'Rubbish,' Seb said confidently. 'You're a warm, perceptive, caring woman. It's just that you're...' His voice trailed off.

She looked up. 'Go on, say what you were going to.'

Seb started to laugh. 'A *really* bad communicator.'

She had no choice but to laugh with him. 'OK, Mr Man of the People,' she said finally when Seb had finished laughing. 'What do you suggest I do about Pete?'

'Give it to him straight—he's got to be told he won't get anywhere until he tries harder because the prof will just let him carry on as he is until Pete misses the promotion boat again. You're better off laying down the law and hopefully Pete will start toeing the line.'

Lucinda by now was only half listening. At that moment she couldn't have cared less about Pete or the professor. The long day had finally caught up with her and the thought of sleeping held far more charm. She put up her hand to stifle a yawn. 'I'm exhausted.'

'Rest, then,' Seb said simply. He kicked the door shut

and, stretching out on the bed, pulled her into his arms. Too tired to resist and so tempted by his touch, she slipped off her shoes and lay back against him. And though he didn't kiss her or try anything—both knew it was neither the time nor place—Lucinda had never felt such an over-whelming feeling of rightness and peace as she lay there in his arms. Her eyes heavy, she glanced at the bedside clock. Eleven minutes past twelve—she wanted to remember the time and the day. After all it would go down in her history as the day that both Bianca and herself had been given a new beginning.

The smell of fresh coffee and a gentle kiss from Seb awoke her. Lucinda responded warmly but, suddenly aware she hadn't brushed her teeth for ages, then she pulled away and stretched luxuriously.

'What time is it?'

Seb smiled. 'Six. I thought you said you were an incur-able insomniac? You snored all night.'

'I did not,' she said indignantly, glad of the darkened room as she felt herself blush.

'I'm only teasing, but you did sleep well. Chocolate for breakfast?'

'There'll be none left for Billy.' Lucinda laughed as she peeled off the wrapper. 'My mother would never forgive me if she saw me now.'

'In a strange man's room?' Seb said jokingly.

'Oh, no, she wouldn't give a hoot about that—it's the chocolate that would worry her. I'll need to go on a diet at this rate. Queensland's only a few weeks away and if I start putting on weight she'll never let me hear the last of it.'

'But you're perfect. What on earth would you need to go on a diet for?'

'As I said last night, you haven't met my mother. Nobody's perfect to her—there's always room for improvement.'

Seb's hand teasingly pulled her theatre top. 'The only improvement you need is to get rid of this,' he said huskily.

'I couldn't agree more, and that's exactly what I intend to do. But in the shower—alone,' she added laughingly. 'Is anyone out there?' Seb opened the door slightly and peered out.

'No, the coast is clear.' She brushed past him but he stopped her in the doorway and pulled her toward him. 'I'll see you later.' As he kissed her, so heady was his embrace she forgot about not brushing teeth and kissed him back.

'Now I know what they mean when they say, "Take a cold shower,"' she joked. 'You're not very good for my blood pressure, Doctor.'

But she didn't take a cold shower. Instead, she took her time relishing the warm water on her skin, recalling the tenderness she had felt wrapped in Seb's arms. Dropping a two-dollar coin in the honesty box, she unwrapped a toothbrush and, after rinsing her mouth, was tempted to go back and kiss him all over again, but common sense won. There would be time for all that later.

After a brief meeting with the professor and Pete, who was looking decidedly seedy, it was decided that Professor Hays would assist Pete in Theatre that morning, leaving Lucinda with the task of catching up on yesterday's work. Lucinda would also see the patients pre-operatively to assess any changes and answer any last-minute questions that arose.

Despite wanting to see Bianca, Lucinda bypassed the PICU, knowing that once she went in there it would be a long time before she could get away. She arrived on the cardiac ward just as the nursing staff were changing over. Ann was looking more harassed than usual.

'I'll be right with you.' Ann finished checking the controlled drugs with another nurse and joined her. 'Sorry about that. We're two nurses down—one's rung in sick and heaven knows where Ellen is. Apparently we're over budget with agency staff so Admin has said we'll have to make do. I wonder if they'd be so pedantic about budgets if it was one of their children having cardiac surgery this morning.'

Her uniform dishevelled, her hair unbrushed, Ellen flew into the ward.

'Sorry I'm late, Sister.'

Ann gave a tight smile. 'You look as if you should be going off duty, not coming on, Ellen.'

'I know. I'm sorry. We had a late night. Pete—'

'I'm not interested,' Ann snapped. 'Go to the staffroom and get a cup of strong coffee, and while you're there how about you make yourself look a bit more professional?' She dismissed the young nurse and walked to the nurses' station with Lucinda. 'Silly girl,' she said huffily. 'She could go far if she put her head down. Too many parties and not enough early nights.'

For her boyfriend, too, Lucinda reflected, but didn't say anything. No wonder Pete was looking so awful. How could he? she wondered furiously. How could he be out on the tiles the night before his big break? If he carried on like this he might as well kiss his career goodbye. She would have to say something, Lucinda decided. As soon as Theatre was over she would have a strong word or two with Pete.

Bianca was doing incredibly well. After a long discussion with the staff, it was decided to attempt to extubate her that afternoon, a little bit earlier than the ideal, but she had already had an ET tube in since Saturday, and if she needed to be ventilated for much longer she would have to have a tracheostomy.

Lucinda's anger at Pete abated somewhat throughout the morning. The patients all returned from Theatre with their notes meticulously written up by Pete, and the word going around was that he had operated beautifully. Somewhat mollified and prepared to discuss things rationally, she made her way to the theatres at lunchtime to be told that Pete was in the coffee-room. Her good-will flew out of the window, though, at the site that confronted her. Pale and sweaty, he was hunched over the sink with the taps running.

'Next time take more water with it.'

Pete splashed his face with water and deliberately turned the taps off before slowly turning around to face her.

'What exactly do you mean by that?'

'You know very well. What on earth were you doing out till all hours at a party the night before you operate? The biggest break of your career and you almost blew it.'

'Ah, but I didn't blow it. Surgery actually went very well this morning, thank you for asking.'

Lucinda ignored his sarcasm.

'Thank God it did, Pete. These are children's lives we're dealing with. This isn't a motor repair garage. You make a mistake here and there might not be a chance to fix it.'

'You think I don't know that?' he shouted.

'Well, act like it, then, Pete. You've got a reputation around this hospital and if you want anyone to start taking you seriously you'd better get rid of it.'

'And you'd know all about reputations, wouldn't you, Miss Chambers? You unfeeling bitch.'

Lucinda stepped back as if she'd been hit.

'How dare you?'

'No, how dare you? You march in here and practically accuse me of being drunk on the job. You've had it in for me since Saturday. The great Miss Chambers examines a patient who promptly arrests. It's not Bianca you're upset about, just the fact you might have missed something. Well, don't take it out on me. Anyway, there was nothing to miss, there was nothing to find. Your excellent medical reputation remains unblemished. And just because you don't have a life outside this hospital doesn't mean the rest of us have to act like confirmed bachelors and spinsters.'

'Well, at least it means I can keep my mind on the job,' she retorted furiously. She was angry with him, of course, but also genuinely concerned. Pete *was* a good doctor, but he was going to lose everything. She needed to take Seb's advice and bring him into line. 'Sometimes you just have to be single-minded to get what you want. I didn't get to be a consultant by trying to juggle relationships with work. They just don't mix, and the sooner you see that the better you'll do.'

Pete shook his head, his eyes narrowing. 'I almost feel sorry for you. You're so hell-bent on your career, there's no room for anyone or anything else. But I tell you this much, I feel sorrier for any guy who tries to get too close to you—he'd need an ice-pick to get through the front door.'

He left smartly and as Lucinda's eyes followed him angrily she almost jumped out of her skin to see Seb standing at the door.

'How long have you been there?' she asked in a shaking voice.

He stared at her for what seemed an age. 'Long enough. I was down here to check on my annual leave and I could hear you two halfway down the corridor. When you give someone a piece of your mind, you certainly don't mince your words, do you, Lucinda?'

Lucinda paled. Still shaking with temper, she frantically

tried to remember exactly what she had said. 'I know I sounded harsh but I was just trying to make a point. It has nothing to do—'

But he cut short her pleas. 'You sounded very convincing to me.'

Before she could argue the point he had gone, leaving Lucinda standing white and thin-lipped. Trembling, she sat on one of the chairs. What a mess, what a sorry mess, and just when things had been going so well, too. But surely when Seb calmed down he would realise what he had overheard had been an argument? That the words she had spoken had been for Pete's benefit, not his? With a groan she placed her head in her hands. The truth was, it didn't matter at whom the words had been directed. Seb had heard her innermost fears today. How could she give Seb and Billy what they both needed? How could she juggle a ready-made family with her work? They had already had one career-minded woman in their lives, and look how that had worked out. Why would Seb risk it again?

Reluctantly she replayed the argument in her mind. Pete had been right, she conceded, well, partly. Some of her anger with him *did* indeed stem from Bianca and her own guilt about Saturday night, but Pete had had no right to speak to her like that, no right at all.

He had every right, she soon found out. Back on the ward she found Ann and asked for a run-down on the post-operative patients.

'All stable. Ellen's looking after the high-dependency patients. I think she had a couple of IV orders but the resident's sorted them out.'

'Ellen's on the high-dependency unit?' Lucinda queried the wisdom behind this decision. But Ann didn't respond as the young nurse herself came over.

'All their obs are good. James White is on his second

unit of packed cells and when that's through the resident needs to review him. They want him to have some Lasix before we put up the third unit. I've handed over to the late staff. I thought I might go and grab a late lunch, if that's all right?'

'Why don't you go home, Ellen, grab an afternoon nap? I think you've more than earned it. We're pretty up to date and now the late shift are here I'm sure we can cover.'

Lucinda raised her eyebrows at Ann's maternal tones.

'Well, if you're sure…'

'Off you go, love,' Ann said kindly, and the young nurse gratefully departed.

'You've changed your tune,' Lucinda remarked once she was out of earshot.

'I had to eat a huge slice of humble pie for my morning coffee-break.' Ann gave an ashamed smile. 'Apparently, Pete had a bit of stage fright in the night. It would seem he's not as cool as he makes out. Poor Ellen spent the night "walking" through the operations with him. She said he went into such detail she feels she could have performed the surgery herself. So I let her put her newfound knowledge to the test and she passed with flying colours. Seems I misjudged her—Pete, too, for that matter. By all accounts he did a great job in Theatre this morning.' She turned and caught sight of Lucinda's worried frown. 'What's wrong?'

'That humble pie you ate this morning,' Lucinda said remorsefully. 'Is there any left?'

Pete, of course, wasn't anywhere to be seen, so Lucinda had to resort to leaving a message with the switchboard to page him and ask him to come to her office. He entered after a brief knock and his temper obviously hadn't abated.

'What's the problem? Hadn't you finished turning the knife?'

'Sit down, please, Pete,' she said calmly.

He did as he was asked and she took a deep breath. 'I owe you an apology, Pete—a big one. I just assumed you were out last night, partying. I had no right to infer that you had been drinking. I know now that I was wrong on both counts. You were also right about Bianca Moore. I was trying to somehow lessen the guilt I feel by dragging you into it when the truth is that no one was to blame. I truly am sorry for the things that I said.'

She held her breath, wondering what his reaction would be, and when she finally dared to look up at him she saw that he was smiling.

'Apology accepted.' He held out his hand over the table and Lucinda shook it.

'And now it's my turn. You were wrong about a lot of things but not all. I feel as guilty as hell about Bianca but, unlike you, I have reason to. Maybe there was nothing to be found but I still should have examined her. And in truth the only reason I was on the ward in the first place was because of Ellen. It's been a huge wake-up call.'

Lucinda relaxed back in the chair. 'So I've got a reputation as a sour old spinster?' Pete shifted uncomfortably. 'It's OK,' she said. 'I did know that was the general consensus of opinion.'

'You don't deserve it.'

'Why not?'

'Pizza and slushy films with Bianca, and I've been going to Suriyan's for years and never seen a competition running.'

'Who told you about that?' Lucinda asked.

'Janine Stewart has been telling everyone. It did her the world of good, and there's not been too many light moments in that woman's life recently, let me tell you.' He paused for a moment. 'So what about my reputation?'

'Pete, it's just a few things I heard, and from what I can

tell now it's totally unfounded, but it must have started somewhere.'

Pete nodded. 'I ran a bit wild when I was a medical student and then when I was an intern it went a bit to my head. But, hell, I was only in my twenties. Ellen and I have been together for two years now. We're deadly serious but everyone just seems to think it's just another fling. I want to get engaged—that would shut them up—but then I wonder if I would be getting engaged for the right reasons. I don't want the hospital to come into it. I want it to be about us.'

Lucinda pondered his dilemmas. 'What I said before about relationships and work not mixing—well, I was referring to the more transient kind. Heaven knows, this job would be a thousand times easier if there was a sympathetic ear to bend at the end of a long day. I'm presuming that's the case, of course. As you so well pointed out, I don't have a lot of experience where relationships are concerned.'

Pete squirmed in his seat and Lucinda gave him an amicable smile to show there were no hard feelings before she continued. 'Pete, you know as well as I do that mud sticks. You have to not only be careful but be seen to be careful. There's a lot of people watching.'

Pete shrugged. 'Not any more,' he said dejectedly. 'You were right about that as well. I did want this job, but at the end of the day you were the better doctor. I can see that now.'

Lucinda shook her head. 'Not better, just a bit more experienced. Your time will come.'

'But when?' he said gloomily.

'When you least expect it probably. Something will come up.'

There was a knock at the door and Pete stood up to leave.

'Friends?' He offered his hand again and Lucinda stood up and shook it warmly.

'Friends.'

As he left Seb entered. 'G'day, Pete, how's things?'

Pete grinned. 'Better. How's your son?'

'Better, too. I just popped in to pick your boss's brains about him, actually.'

'Well, I'll leave you to it.'

Pete closed the door behind him and as Seb turned to face Lucinda she felt her insides melt. The anger was gone from his eyes and she saw again the man who had gently woken her that morning.

'I'm sorry I walked out on you earlier,' he rasped, and as if he couldn't bear the distance between them he crossed the room and took her in his arms, his mouth fervently searching for hers. For a while their minds concentrated on the moment as their lips mingled sensually, the doubts that plagued them both temporarily a million miles away. But as the kiss slowly ended the world rushed in.

'You wanted to see me about Billy?' she asked, pulling away, her voice suddenly concerned. 'Is there anything wrong?'

Seb shook his head. 'Just an excuse. Billy's going great guns this morning. I see you've made up with Pete?' he added.

'Pete and I are fine now,' she said with a mischievous glint in her eye. 'And thanks for your advice by the way— it nearly landed me in court for defamation of character.'

'I never said you had to go that far,' he said contritely, but Lucinda just laughed.

'Enough about Pete. I'm more interested in Billy. How's he coping without Gemma?' Lucinda probed, then held her breath, worried she might have intruded too far. But Seb didn't seem concerned by her question.

'He's coping. Hopefully things are going to start picking up for him now, and not just with his health.' He paused a moment, his eyes narrowing as if he was weighing up whether or not to go any further. Lucinda held her breath until slowly Seb started to open up to her.

'Gemma and I had a long chat yesterday before she left, and for the first time in ages we actually got somewhere.'

Lucinda listened intently, hoping he would elaborate.

'I know it's hard to understand—it's taken me five years—but I finally think I'm starting to.' He sat down and then continued slowly, choosing his words carefully. 'She's not a terrible person. She's just not cut out for motherhood and, being here, she feels as if everyone's judging her, and for once even I can understand where she's coming from. I mean, it's hardly orthodox, a mother walking out on her own child. I was aghast when she decided to move so far away, but now…' He looked up at Lucinda. 'She's actually a better mother. Now the responsibility's gone, now that she can concentrate on her career and all that, she's actually got more to give Billy.'

Lucinda sat there quietly for a moment. 'It must be hard,' she said finally. 'She's made out to be the Wicked Witch of the West just because she's a woman. Nobody bats an eyelid when a man walks out on his children. I'm not condoning it, for either sex, but I guess it's just not as clear-cut as it seems.'

'There is something else I need to talk about, Lucinda.' He held her hands as he spoke. 'I know you were only talking in the heat of a row before, but what you said isn't that far off the mark.' She opened her mouth to protest but Seb held her hands tightly and shook his head. 'Let me finish.'

Nodding silently, she watched with growing trepidation

as he searched for the right words to say. 'We're not going to be able to see much of each other for a while.'

So she had blown it after all. Pulling her hands free, she went and sat down. Picking up a paperweight, Lucinda focussed on the prism of colours in a desperate attempt to keep her composure—there would be time for tears after he had gone. But as Seb continued to speak, hope surged in her again as she realised he wasn't giving up on them, just voicing the problems they both faced.

'As sure as I am of my feelings for you, we've got a lot to work out before we go public, so to speak. We *both* have to be sure before I introduce you into Billy's life. Not just sure of our feelings, but how we're going to work this. I don't want to sound chauvinist, and I honestly don't think I am, but I swore I'd never get involved with another career-minded woman, and look what I've gone and done.' He gave a small smile and Lucinda managed a wobbly one back.

'I'm not saying you're like Gemma...'

'I know,' she admitted, replacing the paperweight on her desk.

'But Billy's been through hell. I don't have the luxury of taking risks and following my heart. So while he's recovering I'm going to have to lie a bit low. We'll see each other at the hospital once I'm back at work, of course, and I can ring. I just think it's too early to be openly going out. You do understand, don't you?'

Lucinda nodded; it was something she had already thought long and hard about. Part of her wanted to tell him the truth, that she wasn't sure if she even wanted her career, but how could she? If she let her feelings be known and things didn't work out between them, she would have potentially committed career suicide, for even the vaguest hint that she wasn't devoted to her work would see her passed over for promotion—Pete Hughes was living proof of that. As private a person as Seb was, to tell him she was having doubts about her job could place her in a very vulnerable position. And anyway it was far too early to be making such huge declarations. It might scare him off.

She gave him a reassuring smile. 'Of course I understand,' she said honestly. 'It's difficult enough for us to comprehend the speed at which things have happened. I can only imagine how hard it would be for a child. There's no rush. Billy has to come first.' She saw the relief wash over his face. 'Look, Seb, I have to go over to PICU now. They're going to extubate Bianca and I'd like to be there.'

'Sure, and, Lucinda, thank you for understanding.' And as he pulled her into his arms and his lips met hers she knew she could hold on for as long as it was needed. Some things were worth waiting for.

And so they took it gently, very gently. Their work schedules hardly allowed for anything else. But they would grab a coffee in the canteen and sometimes breakfast and catch up on each other's lives until invariably one or the other was called away. The problems that had surfaced were still there, waiting in the wings, but they were put on hold for a while as Lucinda and Seb got to know each other better. And while the rest of the hospital remained oblivious to the scandal that was evolving—and by hospital standards this really was a plum piece of gossip—in Theatre she would check the whiteboard each morning and her heart would soar or sink depending upon which anaesthetist had been allocated to her.

Seb, Lucinda soon found out at first hand, was indeed a skilled and competent anaesthetist, and despite her desire to see him for more personal reasons, Lucinda also enjoyed working alongside him on professional grounds, secure in the knowledge her patients were receiving the best of attention.

As Professor Hays had pointed out on Lucinda's first day, Seb did indeed talk to his anaesthetised patients. In his pre-op checks he would find out their interests, and on Seb's operation notes you could always find a brief summary of a child's hobbies. She grew used to listening to Seb nattering away about the football scores or the latest pop groups. 'They can't hear you,' she pointed out during one long operation. 'And if they can, you're not doing your job properly.'

But Seb had just smiled and carried on chatting, his passion for the patient's individuality a constant reminder to all that they weren't just dealing with numbers here, but precious children.

And despite the restraints of work and his family, they somehow managed a few stolen kisses in her office, and late at night when Billy was asleep he would try to ring. As hard as it was, living in limbo, Lucinda was in a strange way grateful for the reprieve. The depth of her feelings enthralled and terrified her. She was considering taking on an awesome responsibility in Seb and Billy—it was a lot to think about.

CHAPTER SIX

PETE HUGHES, once the animosity had gone, over the next few weeks became a wonderful friend as well as colleague. Now Lucinda trusted him implicitly, and the more responsibility she gave him the better surgeon he became. They spent the time between theatre cases whiling the time away with idle chit-chat and Pete filled her in on the hospital gossip.

'Ellen's lingering a bit too long over the jewellery catalogues,' he mentioned one lunchtime.

'So why don't you go ahead? Lucinda asked.

Pete gave a shrug. 'I'm not against marriage as such. It's just, well, my parents are divorced and so is my brother. And working in this place, it's hardly an advertisement for the institution of marriage. Everyone seems to be playing the field—the divorce rate around here is terrifying.'

Lucinda mused over this. 'It is pretty scary.' She hesitated. 'Look at Seb and his ex-wife.' The chance to talk about him to gain some insight was too tempting to pass up. But Pete shook his head.

'That was one marriage that didn't end because of an affair—well, definitely not on Seb's part and I'm pretty sure Gemma didn't have one. That really would have been the last straw. Seb would never have put up with that and he put up with enough, let me tell you.'

'Like what?' Lucinda said casually, trying not to sound too interested.

'Well…' Pete had a brief look around the theatre coffee-room to be sure no one was listening. 'I think they were happy until Gemma got pregnant. Apparently she was devastated but Seb was pleased, I was only junior then but he bought everyone cigars and was grinning from ear to ear. Anyway, Gemma just didn't want to know. She'd never wanted children but everyone thought that once the baby came along she'd change her mind. But it only made her more adamant.'

'Maybe she had postnatal depression?' Lucinda ventured, but Pete shook his head.

'She just didn't want a child. She wanted her career. She's in advertising or something and the fact Billy was ill only made things worse.'

'But how do you know all this?' Lucinda asked. 'Seb strikes me as a really private person. How come everyone knows all the details?'

'Because poor Seb had no choice but to tell. Gemma just carried on as if she didn't have a baby. I was doing my surgical rotation when Billy was a baby, and most of my lunches in this room were taken with one of the nurses feeding Billy because the nanny had resigned or Billy was too unwell to go to day care. Billy was brought up here, and if it wasn't the theatre staff feeding him, he was tucked in a bassinet in Ann Benton's office. Everyone likes Seb and they were only too happy to help.

'Anyway, Seb finally drew the line, said it was ridiculous. He'd be better off on his own. At least he and Billy would know where they stood. Gemma was only to happy to relinquish any responsibility, and now she's living in Sydney.'

Lucinda took it all in, her face portraying only the usual interest she would have shown at any hospital gossip, but her heart sank. What Seb must have been through didn't bear thinking about. How, she tried to fathom, did he manage to be so civil to her? No wonder the nursing staff had been hostile towards Gemma.

'Not very pleasant, is it?' Pete concluded, then turned the subject back to work. 'Are you looking forward to the medical conference?'

She gave a half-smile and nodded, but inside her heart soared.

Queensland was only a few days away and Lucinda had already packed. Dashing out to the shops on her lunch-break, she had purchased some flattering clothes and the thought of two days with Seb made her toes curl. She knew they would be busy but still...

'Lucinda, there you are. I've been paging you?' Jack Wells popped his head around the door.

Lucinda gave a small frown as she checked her pager. 'My batteries are flat. I'd better call Switchboard.' She picked up the phone on the coffee-table. 'What did you want to see me about, Jack?'

'Billy Carlisle has been admitted from Casualty to the chest medical ward.'

Lucinda hastily replaced the telephone. 'He's what?' she said, alarmed. 'What's wrong?'

Pete's eyebrows shot up in surprise at her response as Jack filled her in on the details.

'A chest infection, and possibly gastro. He's all right, though. Vince Cole, the respiratory consultant, thought that we should have a look, though, given he's only a few weeks post-op. I thought I should let you know, what with his dad being a doctor here. It might be better if a consultant takes a look at Billy.'

Lucinda, realising she had completely overreacted, gave a casual smile, though her heart was racing. 'Sure, I'll be right down.' She picked up her stethoscope and went to leave.

'Shouldn't you let Switchboard know about your pager?' Pete asked.

'Of course. Could you ring the ward and get them to organise an echocardiogram?'

'He's already had one in Casualty—the results are up on the ward.'

By the time she had rung Switchboard and collected a new pager, Lucinda was nearly beside herself. She knew she was probably worrying unnecessarily but, still, with Billy's asthma she just had to see the little guy for herself. A nurse escorted her to the side room and she braced herself to remain professionally cool when she saw Seb, but it was just Billy, sitting by himself on the bed.

'He's not very happy,' the nurse warned her. 'He's completely hospitalised. He wants to go back to his old ward or ''at the very least'' be moved onto the main ward. It's probably not gastro. More than likely the antibiotics are giving him diarrhoea, but until we get his results from Path I don't want to risk him on the main ward.'

Lucinda gave a laugh. 'Fair enough. Hello, Billy.' His miserable face looked up and at the sight of a familiar face broke into a huge grin.

'Miss Chambers.'

'We'll be all right,' she said to the nurse, who nodded gratefully and made her way back to the busy ward.

After examining him thoroughly, Lucinda looked at his X-rays. He had some consolidation on the right lower lobe and his lungs were hyperinflated from the Ventolin. She scanned the echocardiogram results.

'Your heart's working beautifully.'

Billy gave a frown.

'What's wrong? You don't look very pleased. That's good news.'

'Not for me. I want to go back to my old ward, see Ann and my friends.'

'I know, but hopefully once these new antibiotics kick in and you've had some extra fluid through that drip, you'll be home again.'

Billy didn't look very appeased. 'Dad said Bianca's a lot better.'

'That's right. She went home on Monday.'

'Dad said that she got a whole new heart and lungs. That would have saved you a lot of work, I guess.'

'How's that?' she asked.

'Well, you said yourself it was too complicated to fix. I suppose it was much easier just to get a new one.'

His five-year-old logic brought a smile to her lips. 'Well, I'm going to write some notes up. I'll probably come and check on you tomorrow.'

His face fell.

'Dad's gone to the airport to get Mum. I can't get this stupid video to work.' He pushed at the remote control.

'You have to turn the television on first.' Lucinda fiddled with the switches and a huge silver robot appeared on screen.

And Lucinda was never quite sure how it happened, but before she knew it the film had ended and she was now well versed in the hierarchy of the Mega-Galaxy and the battles of the Robot Savers. Lucinda glanced at her watch, yelping when she saw the time.

'I really do have to go now and you, young man, should get some rest.'

He gave a big smile. 'Bye, Miss Chambers.'

'Would you prefer an aisle or window seat?'

'Window, please.'

The flight attendant tapped her request into the computer.

'Travelling alone?'

Lucinda tried to smile. 'I'm not sure. I was supposed to be meeting a colleague here. Has a Dr Sebastian Carlisle checked in yet?'

She continued tapping. 'Not yet. He'd better step on it, they're starting to board. I'll reserve the seat next to you for him if he makes it in time.' With a smile she handed Lucinda back her ticket and gave her her boarding card. 'Have a nice flight.'

Annoyingly, and most unusually, the flight boarded bang on time and with a sigh Lucinda clipped on her seat belt, glancing longingly at the empty seat beside her. All her hopes had been pinned on Queensland and now it looked like Seb wasn't going to make it. She had tried not to build her hopes up, but after the initial panic Billy had responded well to the antibiotics and had been discharged on the Wednesday. Seb, after a lot of thought, had decided to come. Gemma was going to stay with Billy. But he must have changed his mind.

Just as the cabin doors were about to close a flurry of activity made her look up. Seb, slightly breathless, made his way down the aisle, his eyes lighting up when he saw her.

'What happened? Is Billy all right?'

Seb slipped into the seat beside her, his thighs brushing against her as he put his hand luggage under the seat. 'He's great. He and Gemma are armed with videos and popcorn. Couldn't wait to get rid of me. I got stuck with a patient at the hospital.'

'Not one of mine, I hope?'

'Kimberley Stewart. She's had a cerebral bleed.'

'Oh, no, but she was doing so well.'

Seb shook his head. 'Not really, Lucinda. She's never really picked up.'

'How bad is it?'

Seb gave a heavy sigh. 'Bad enough, on top of everything else.'

'Poor Janine and Mark.'

The mood was subdued as the plane taxied along the runway.

'Lucinda, I know it's awful but there's nothing either of us can do from here. We'll be back at work on Monday. You've been working sixty-hour weeks and you need a break. You can't take it with you.'

She knew he was right—of course he was—but as the plane took off she offered a silent prayer for Kimberley and her family. Turning to Seb, she saw his eyes closed and knew he was doing the same.

After lunch had been served the chattering stopped as most of the passengers dozed, but the bliss of being able to talk uninterrupted by pagers and to sit in such close proximity meant that sleep was the last thing on either of their minds. Sipping their gin and tonics, they gradually left behind the world and its problems and concentrated on each other. And slowly Seb filled her in about Gemma. It was exactly as Pete had described it, but hearing it from Seb made her eyes fill with tears for what they had been through.

'But how do you manage to stay civil to her?' she asked.

'That took a while, but she is Billy's mother. It's not as easy as just washing your hands and saying that's it.' He looked at her confused face. 'Gemma's not a bad person, we had a happy marriage at first. We were young and apart from work there were no responsibilities. I guess it was easy to be happy then. She was so upset when she found out she was pregnant, but I just assumed she'd come round. I never really took her doubts seriously.'

'But she didn't come round.'

Seb took a sip of his drink. 'No,' he said sadly. 'She tried, I'll give her that, but it just wasn't her. I guess some women just shouldn't have children. As I said before, I don't consider myself a chauvinist, but a sixty-hour-a-week job and children just don't mix, to my mind anyway. Something has to give when you're a parent.'

'Why didn't you stop working?' Lucinda asked, playing devil's advocate. 'Become a house husband?'

His eyes narrowed as he considered her words, and Lucinda suddenly realised what he must be thinking—that she was suggesting *he* give up work if they were to ever get together.

'Because as high-flying as Gemma is now, it took a long time and a lot of work before the dollars started rolling in. Someone had to pay the mortgage.' He swirled an ice cube around his drink and Lucinda found herself holding her breath as he continued.

'Maybe I'm more of a chauvinist than I thought,' he admitted honestly. 'I don't know if I'd like to be a house husband. I was always brought up to believe a man worked for a living.'

Lucinda hesitated and then thought, To hell with it. She asked the question whose answer she dreaded the most.

'Do you miss her?'

Seb nearly choked on his drink. 'Hell, no. Look, Lucinda, I did love Gemma but that was a long time ago. I know I seem accepting of her but it's taken me a long time to get there, it's been a hellish five years. Now it's just me and Billy, things are better. Gemma does care and she does love him in her own way—she just isn't cut out for the school runs and tooth-fairy tales. Anyway, there's been too much water under the bridge to even think about giving it another go. All I want from Gemma is for her to treat Billy properly. If she can't be a full-time mother I have to accept that, and I won't make things worse for Billy by rowing with her, but I certainly don't love her any more.'

'But what if she changed?' Lucinda insisted. 'What if she decides she wants Billy and you later on?'

Seb's face darkened and it was the first time Lucinda had heard any animosity in his voice. It made the hairs on her neck stand up.

'She'll never get him back, I made sure of that when I got full custody, I won't have Billy messed around again. And as for me, how could I love her again after seeing the pain she's caused my son?'

He took another long drink and for a second stared beyond her out of the plane window, but Lucinda knew he wasn't taking in the view. He turned back to her and his face was smiling. That conversation was definitely over.

'Where do your parents live?' he asked.

'In Noosa. I'll probably take a taxi and meet them for lunch on Sunday before we head back.'

'How's your speech going?' Seb gave a grimace. 'Do you know John McClelland? He's the bald guy a few rows in front, works at Ballarat City.'

Lucinda shook her head.

'We've both been doing similar research and we're going to do the presentation together. We were supposed to brainstorm it this week, but with Billy being sick we didn't get round to it. I'm going to have to do a lot of work with him tonight.'

Lucinda felt a stab of disappointment.

'Which gives us most of Saturday. Once my speech is out of the way I'm all yours. Anyway, we can hardly hole ourselves up in our room the whole time.'

'Why not?' Lucinda grumbled, then smiled. 'OK, never let it be said I stood in the way of your career.' A look she couldn't interpret flashed over Seb's face and for a second Lucinda wondered what she had said wrong, but as she continued speaking his face broke into another smile. 'John can have you tonight but then it's my turn.'

If Lucinda had had any romantic ideas of a cosy weekend for the two of them, her illusions were hastily shattered when they arrived at the luxurious beachside hotel. After checking in, she was shown to her room. After reading the itinerary, she realised that all of their time there was pretty much accounted for.

The afternoon was taken up with formal lectures, followed by dinner and then back for a group discussion. The following morning was packed again, with a break after lunch for some leisure time and then more lectures. There were even lectures on Sunday morning, though only until eleven. The rest of the day was free with further conferences in the evening. However, that didn't apply to her and Seb as they were leaving. No wonder Professor Hays had seemed so delighted when he'd said he couldn't attend. Oh, well. Lucinda shrugged. It was her first medical conference as a consultant and she was determined to enjoy it.

A welcoming basket of tropical fruit was on the table and Lucinda helped herself to a pawpaw. There was also a small wicker basket containing shampoo and conditioner and various bath and body oils, even a few condoms. The Plaza, it seemed, catered for everyone.

Making her way down to the conference room, she stood at the door uneasily for a moment. Seb was nowhere to be seen and most of the faces were new to her. Assuming a confident pose, Lucinda hovered on the edge of the most familiar-looking group, desperately hoping to be included in the conversation. Seb was still nowhere in sight, she realised miserably, then kicked herself. The last thing she wanted was to look as if she needed rescuing.

'We haven't been introduced. The name's Jeremy Foster. I'm a consultant surgeon at Melbourne City.'

Lucinda turned grateful to have someone to talk to.

'Lucinda Chambers. I'm at the Women's and Children's.'

'I know. I've heard a lot about you and what I don't already know I intend to find out.'

Lucinda nearly choked. Well, he didn't waste any time. She took in the blond looks and sultry eyes. He was good-looking, but not to her taste. And he was about as subtle as a sledgehammer. Still, at least it was someone to talk to.

'Are you giving a talk here?' she asked politely.

'Not this time. I'm actually working on designing a new instrument but it's rather early days to be presenting it.' And he was off. Over the next fifteen minutes Jeremy Foster gave her an in-depth description of his idea, which to Lucinda's mind was nothing particularly new or exciting anyway. The only reason he would be doing it, she knew, was to put his name to something, but she listened politely or at least pretended to. The occasional 'hmm' or 'really' was all the encouragement he needed to talk about himself.

'Hello, there, Jeremy, Lucinda.' Seb greeted them both and Lucinda gave a relieved smile.

'Hello, there, Sebastian. Haven't seen you in ages, though I must make a point of following up a couple of the referrals I pass your way if your hospital's latest acquisition is anything to go by.' His eyes flicked knowingly to Lucinda.

Seb gave him a cool smile, 'And I thought we were here to discuss medicine.'

Thankfully Jeremy took his cue and left them to it.

'What did he want?' Seb asked, sounding irritated.

'To talk about himself,' Lucinda replied lightly, glad that Seb seemed rattled. 'How's your room?'

'Too far from yours. Hell, I hate these things. Everyone trying to outdo each other, full of their own self-importance. If you weren't here I'd be tempted to catch the next plane home.'

'You're speaking, remember.'

'How could I forget? John's getting worked up. Apparently a couple of the bigwigs from his hospital are here.'

'I don't blame him for being worked up. This is the big league here, real make-or-break stuff. Sorry. I'm probably not helping.'

Seb shook his head. 'I couldn't give a damn. I'm not out to impress, just to learn something and hopefully share what I've been researching.'

That was so like him, Lucinda thought. Seb was easily as knowledgeable as anyone in this room yet he didn't let it go to his head. His concern was always his patients. Resisting the urge to reach out and touch him, instead she took a sip of her drink. It was hell being so close and not able to do a thing about it.

'C'mon. You can show me your room. The lectures don't start for another half-hour.' He must have read her mind.

And finally they were alone, and those brief moments were all it took to convey the urgency of their feelings and sustain her until tomorrow. He took her hand and led her to the king-sized bed. Gently he laid her down and stretched out beside her, his hand gently exploring her body through her flimsy dress and coming to rest on her breast as he kissed her deeply, his hand becoming more insistent as her nipples swelled beneath his expert touch. With a low moan she arched her body towards him, and despite the unwelcome restraints of their clothes she could feel the solid weight of his desire against her trembling thighs.

'We're like a couple of teenagers,' Lucinda gasped a few moments later, 'creeping away for a necking session.'

Seb reluctantly pulled away. 'Shall we put the "Do Not Disturb" sign on the door and play a bit of hookey, then?'

It was tempting, very tempting, but they both knew it was impossible. Finally they stood up, straightening their clothes.

'Do you want to go down first? I'll follow in a couple of minutes.'

'I'm sick of playing games,' he said suddenly. 'We've nothing to be ashamed of and after this weekend the whole world's going to know anyway.' And purposefully he took her hand and walked out with her to the lift. They made their way down the stairs, their hands entwined. Never had she felt more proud or confident.

The stolen moments in her room and the public display of affection made the rest of the day more bearable. Oh, she longed to be near him, longed to whisk him away from John McClelland and upstairs, but she had waited this long so she could wait a bit more.

And when on Saturday morning he stood up with John to deliver the lecture she knew she had been right to be patient. They were superb. Seb, being the more senior, went into considerable depth about their subject while John backed it up with the statistics and results. But it was Seb who somehow delivered a human touch, allowing the personalities of his subjects to shine through, which made for riveting listening. Suddenly he held the room in the palm of his hand as he spoke of the reduced pain, the increased mobility, fewer chest infections.

Lucinda knew he had done what he had to set out to do. Knew that everyone in this room would go back to their various roles and see where paediatric pain-controlled analgesia could be implemented. The thunderous applause that followed made her heart swell with pride. Seb and John were the men of the moment and Lucinda was more than happy to take a back seat.

Throughout the day various doctors accosted him, and though he spoke to them politely Lucinda was ever aware of his hungry eyes on her.

Finally, though, the lectures were over. Seeing Seb holed up with John and a few cronies, she escaped to the pool to do some laps.

'We meet again.' She surfaced, pushing her hair out of her eyes. Jeremy Foster gave her the benefit of a very wide smile.

'Well, as we're staying at the same hotel it's hardly much of a surprise.' Lucinda said, somewhat irritated.

'Do you fancy a drink?'

Lucinda shook her head. 'If I have to look at that bar again, I think I'll go,' she said truthfully, then kicked herself as she realised she had given him an opening and men like Jeremy rarely missed a chance.

'Who said anything about going to the bar?' He gave her a seductive smile. 'I've got a well-stocked mini-bar in my room just waiting to be raided.'

Lucinda was used to being chatted up, and normally she could brush unwelcome advances off easily, but this man had skin as thick as rhino's hide. Suddenly she became angry. Just what did he take her for? Did he really think she would go upstairs with him?

'Well, you'd better get used to drinking alone,' she snapped, and in one lithe movement she hauled herself out of the pool. Wrapping her sarong tightly around her, she made her way to her room.

Gibbering with rage at his unwelcome advances, she peeled off her bathers, only to hear a firm rap on the door.

'Go away,' she shouted.

'Lucinda?' Hearing Seb's voice, she grabbed her sarong and tied it around her waist, before opening the door.

'What's wrong?' he demanded. 'I'm sorry I couldn't get away sooner but I'm here now.'

'It's not you,' she said, pulling him in. After having a brief look down the corridor, she closed the door.

'I thought we weren't in hiding any more?'

'We're not, just me. That Jeremy Foster really is insatiable.'

'Has he been giving you a hard time?' Seb frowned. He was wearing only a beach towel draped around his waist. 'Do you want me to have a word?'

'I can take care of myself, thanks. I just gave him an extremely cold shoulder. For a moment, though, I thought he'd followed me up here.'

'Wouldn't put it past him—that guy has broken more hearts than you've fixed. I saw him eyeing you up. Bloody lech.'

'Seb.' Lucinda laughed. 'You weren't jealous, were you?'

'No,' he said, then shrugged. 'Well, maybe a little bit, I guess. I was just coming down to the pool to join you for a swim. I've spent the last twenty-four hours with you looking completely stunning and haven't been able to do a thing about it.'

'Until now,' she said huskily.

'Until now.' he replied, his eyes glazing over with lust. 'Come here.'

Seductively she undid her sarong and it slithered to the ground. His eyes travelled searchingly over her body, melting her with his gaze. Slowly she walked over to him, her hands reaching out and touching his broad chest, her long nails dragging teasingly around his nipples then slowly working their way down. She undid the towel and purposefully she slipped off his bathers with one hand as the other boldly explored the delicious beauty of his malehood.

His lips nuzzled her shoulders, soft hot kisses, her satin skin fragrant with the scent of desire, mingling with the pool's chlorine. Moving downwards, ever downwards, his searching mouth found her glorious heavy breasts and with a low moan he buried his head in their velvet softness.

'Lucinda, oh, Lucinda,' he rasped, his voice deep and breathless. Scooping her up in his strong arms, he carried her over to the bed, his mouth never leaving hers. As he tenderly laid her down they both trembled violently. His mouth hadn't finished exploring her yet and he searched relentlessly as she lay beneath him, squirming in ecstasy until she could take it no more.

Gasping with pleasure, she leant over and with shaking hands she wrestled with the foil package that was their final obstacle. Achingly slowly, firm and then gentle, she unravelled the thin latex along the long length of him, and then there was nothing that could stop them and he dived into her depths.

Like two lost souls that had always belonged together, they began their journey, each knowing instinctively the way to go, pushing each other on, pulling each other back, climbing slowly with sudden bursts of energy that brought them nearer. Until finally, exhausted and gasping, they reached the peak in perfect unison, holding each other tightly as the world rushed by around them.

'I've wanted you for so long,' he said finally as they lay in each other's arms, their long limbs entwined. As she gazed into his loving eyes Lucinda finally knew what it felt to be loved.

Later as they bathed together in the huge spa and he slowly soaped her thighs, the dispersing bubbles displayed her breasts so invitingly that Seb seductively moved his hand slowly higher and to her gasps of surprise and delight he took her there and then in the water.

Drying her slowly, his strong hands massaging her through the soft towel, Seb laughed as he caught sight of the empty basket 'We've exhausted the hotel's supplies.'

'Well, I'm not ringing housekeeping to ask for more condoms.' Lucinda said, blushing at the thought.

'We'll just have to move up to my room, then.'

As good as they were, the evening's lectures were wasted on Lucinda and Seb. Trying hard to concentrate, she was all too aware of Seb next to her. She could smell his newly washed hair, feel his thighs next to hers, and she was tempted to take him by the hand and run back up to her room. But they got through and finally when the meal was over and they had stayed for one drink to be polite, they escaped back upstairs, ordering breakfast to be delivered before she succumbed again to his rapturous love-making.

'You're a great cure for my insomnia,' she said finally as she lay completely spent beside him.

He kissed her goodnight slowly, then tucked himself behind her with one arm protectively wrapped around her until she drifted off. And it felt so right he stayed like that all night, not wanting to ever let her go.

CHAPTER SEVEN

As THE Queensland sun streamed through the window, Lucinda felt the delicious glow on her face. In their haste to be together they hadn't drawn the curtains and she lay there half-asleep, feeling the sun on her skin and the warmth of Seb so close next to her. She felt him stir slightly and she nuzzled against him, feeling him rising against her as welcome as the new day, their bodies instinctively reaching out for each other. Effortlessly he slipped inside her and they rocked together. Like a surreal dream, drugged on sleep and lust, they made hazy love.

'What a gorgeous way to wake up,' she said much later, stretching like a cat on the bed.

He ran a warm hand over her breast. 'You look good enough to eat.' He bent his head and tenderly nuzzled at her breasts, but a sharp knock on the door halted him.

'Looks like the real thing's here.' Lucinda laughed as they hastily covered themselves with the sheet.

Without even a glance, the housemaid delivered the breakfast trolley, wheeling it in and with painstaking slowness proceeding to pour the juice.

'We'll take it from here, thanks,' Seb said finally. 'Do you think I was supposed to tip her?' he asked when she'd gone.

'She'd have got a pretty big tip if you'd got out of bed like that,' Lucinda remarked as he stood up.

They feasted on eggs Benedict and guava juice and fed each other strawberries and melon like two newly-weds.

'Let's skip the morning's lectures,' Seb said as they read the papers.

Lucinda gave a shrug. 'All right, but if Professor Hays finds out I'm going to say you corrupted me.'

'I corrupted you?' He laughed. 'I think it was the other way around.' The ringing of the telephone interrupted their cheerful banter. Lucinda answered it and listened carefully as Seb carried on reading.

'We're not going to be missing the lectures,' she said eventually when she replaced the receiver.

'How come?'

'This morning's speaker has gone down with gastro and they've asked me to do it.'

'What's it on?' he asked gently, seeing how pale she had gone.

'Micro-prems.'

'You'll walk it,' he said confidently, but they both knew it was a tough task. Lectures like these took weeks of preparation, but an opportunity to be seen on this floor was just too good to pass up.

Lucinda was an excellent public speaker. Years at a top boarding school and her time at uni on the debating team had seen to that, but as she took the stage she realised this was her toughest audience yet. Although the presenter had thanked her profusely for stepping in at such short notice, and had told the guests the same, the room was packed with the best medical brains and her hastily written notes were sketchy. The only statistics she had to back her up were the ones in her head. She had no slides, no graphs to work with.

Clearing her throat, she started. Seb gave her a reassuring smile and she smiled back hesitantly. Then, like a baby bird stretching its wings, she hopped off the branch and realised she was flying.

'Initially I was sceptical. These babies are barely viable. We put them and their families thorough hell and more often than not to no avail.' She went into the various ailments these babies faced, speaking briefly of cortical blindness from too much oxygen, necrotising encolitis and then in more depth about cardiac defects, arrhythmias and lung immaturity, recalling statistics that had stuck in her head from when she had pondered this subject long into the night. Her depth of knowledge was truly amazing and she held the audience in the palm of her hand as she spoke with wisdom and passion on this most difficult subject.

As she concluded she looked around the room, her eyes staring directly into the enthralled audience. 'Micro-prems aren't my speciality, but neither are they the exclusive property of the neonatologist. It takes a huge combination of skill and experience, involving practically the whole spectrum of specialties, to care for these infants, and each plays a vital role. Pain, too, plays a big part. Are we subjecting these babies to too much pain? A lot of research is being done but we'll never know the complete answer. We heard yesterday from Drs Carlisle and McClelland about the problems of interpreting pain in infants. How must it be for these the tiniest of babies? It is something we must all consider when we subject them to endless procedures in the quest for life.

'As I said, I used to be sceptical, and it used to worry me. I like to know my own opinions, be able to give an assured answer, but I have now realised that on this subject no one can. We are right to be sceptical—the answers to the ethical and medical debates thrown up by these micro-prems remain equivocal. But, like it or not, medical research is advancing and these tiny babies pave the way for ones that come later.' She paused. 'So we will soldier on until such time as a law is passed which dictates a viable delivery age. But we have to tread carefully, we have to inform the parents each step of the way.' She thought of Kimberley, of Janine and Mark.

'Some will say enough is enough and we have to respect that, others will want us to do all we can. We have to respect that, too. But our first priority once a baby is born must be to that child. We, as doctors, have to be their advocates first and foremost, no matter how tough the going gets.'

She took her seat, the applause continued, and Lucinda let out a huge sigh of relief. The presenter thanked her once again for stepping in and then called an end to the morning lectures.

As Lucinda made her way to the bar her peers shook her hand and congratulated her but it was only Seb she wanted to see. Jeremy Foster, ever the optimist, appeared suddenly with two glasses of champagne.

'You were fabulous. I thought you might like to celebrate.'

And then Seb was beside her.

'She was, wasn't she?' He kissed her cheek and, taking the glasses from a furious Jeremy, he handed one to Lucinda. 'How thoughtful of you, Jeremy. Cheers.'

They were still laughing about it as Lucinda waited in the foyer for her taxi.

'You look nervous,' Seb commented. 'I thought you'd be relieved now it's over.'

'They…' she gestured to the bar '…were a piece of cake compared to my parents.'

Seb laughed. 'They can't be all that bad.'

'You don't know them.'

Seb took a deep breath 'Well, that's easily solved.'

'You mean…' Her heart soared at the prospect of him joining her.

'It will take me two minutes to pack. Tell the taxi to wait.'

As the porter loaded their suitcases into the boot John McClelland came to say goodbye and congratulate Lucinda on her speech.

'In all I would say it's been a successful weekend,' he said in a friendly voice as he shook her hand. 'I'll catch you later, Seb, and think seriously about what I said.'

Seb gave him a brief nod and shook his hand. As they climbed into the taxi all thoughts of her lecture vanished as Lucinda contemplated the meeting ahead.

'Don't worry.' Seb squeezed her thigh reassuringly as she sat tensely next to him on the back seat. 'It will only be for a couple of hours—our plane's at two.'

She turned her troubled eyes to him. 'Don't say I didn't warn you.'

Despite Lucinda's hesitancy at introducing Seb to her parents, the initial meeting went well. Seb played along when Abigail insisted on kissing him on both cheeks and Richard patted him on the back like a long-lost son. He also didn't look remotely embarrassed when Abigail kicked up the most terrible fuss at an extremely smart restaurant because she didn't like the table, but Lucinda inwardly cringed.

'*Lucindah*, what on earth have they been feeding you down there? My baby's grown so big, hasn't she, Richard?'

Seb leant back in his chair. 'Your "baby" has just delivered the most marvellous speech on micro-prems with only an hour's notice. She was very impressive.'

Abigail turned to Lucinda.

'Where was the conference held again?'

Lucinda felt her irritation rise—she had already told her mother three times in the hope they'd come and see her. 'The Plaza.'

'That's right, I remember you telling me now. It's *very* nice there. They have a new head chef there, poached from Romeo's. The Merringtons are having their Christmas do there, I'm looking forward to it.'

Lucinda felt her spirits sink. If she was so looking forward to testing the menu why couldn't she have come down this weekend? Lucinda wondered, but, then, the Merringtons were important people, Lucinda reflected, while she was only their daughter.

'So you're an anaesthetist?' Richard finally spoke.

'That's right.'

'Excellent. Where would we all be without a gas man?' He laughed heartily at his stale joke, but Seb joined in.

Abigail studied the menu carefully. 'Everything's fried, or with cream sauce,' she said impatiently. 'I'll have to speak with the chef myself.' She clicked her fingers at a passing waiter.

'Mum, please, there's plenty of choice. What about the barramundi in lime sauce? It sounds delicious.'

'Is that what you're having?'

Lucinda nodded reluctantly, replacing the menu on the table.

'Well, I'm going to have a huge roast with all the trimmings,' Seb said loudly. 'It is Sunday after all.'

Richard chose a grilled flake and after the waiter had received his strict instruction about the salad dressing there was a sticky moment as Richard ordered the drinks.

'We'd better make it two bottles. Is sparkling all right with you, Seb?'

Seb nodded amicably. 'Whatever everyone else is having.'

'We'll have two bottles of sparkling mineral water,' Richard said to the waiter as he finally handed him back the menus.

Seb called the waiter back as he gratefully departed from the difficult table.

'I'll have a beer, thanks,' Seb said pointedly.

Abigail again turned her attention to Lucinda.

'Next time your professor has to go to a wedding and wants you to attend a conference, make sure it's an international one. You need more exposure, Lucinda. You really ought to be pushing for some international experience. London would be good. Have you asked about a second-ment yet?'

'Mum, I've only been there five minutes, for goodness' sake.'

'Doesn't matter. This is no time to be resting on your laurels. Amanda Merrington has just been made Associate Professor, and she was in your year at medical school. Why do you think they've booked the Plaza for their Christmas do? So Phillip and Celeste can ram the happy news down everybody's throats, that's why. Mind you, she's a der-matologist.' She turned to Seb and shuddered visibly. 'I couldn't think of anything worse, could you? What a fright-ful job, looking at all those ugly skin rashes. Yuk.'

To his credit Seb laughed. 'I expect you see a few un-pleasant sights in your job,' he said with good humour, attempting to divert the conversation.

But Abigail wasn't going to be deflected. 'Ah, but not for long. By the time I've finished with them they're per-fect. Now, Lucinda, as I was saying, you mustn't let the grass grow under your feet. You need to get a few articles published—put your name to something, make a bit of noise.'

Thankfully the meals arrived, which managed to stop Abigail's attack as she scrutinised her plate. Lucinda poked at her salad with a fork.

'What are you doing?' Seb said quietly. 'Trying to find

a calorie?' Lucinda gave a small laugh and watched hungrily as Seb tucked unashamedly into his roast. And slowly she started to relax. Her parents were as obnoxious and pretentious as ever throughout the meal, but somehow with Seb here beside her, deflecting the blows, adding a dry touch of humour, her parents didn't seem quite so poisonous. She was actually almost enjoying herself.

'Lucinda,' Abigail said sharply as the dessert trolley was wheeled before them. 'Remember the saying—a moment on the lips, a lifetime on the hips.'

Seb started to laugh. 'You could always give her a free session of liposuction. I'm going to have a huge slice of mud cake. Billy would never forgive me if he found out I passed on dessert. Billy's my son,' he added as Abigail gave him a questioning look.

'You've got a son?' she asked in a horrified voice.

'Seb's divorced. His ex-wife lives in Sydney,' Lucinda hastily explained, and Abigail seemed placated.

'That's all right, then. I expect it's nice when you get up there to see him,' she said in friendlier tones, but her face turned purple when she heard Seb's reply.

'Actually, I've got full custody. It's my ex-wife who does the visiting.'

'I'm just going to the powder room,' Lucinda said, excusing herself and rushing off. Once there she splashed her face with water. She had known Seb would never hide Billy—he was fiercely proud of his son. And after all, she was hardly in her early twenties. Most men of her age had some history. In a funny way she actually felt relieved now everything was out in the open. There was never going to be a good time to tell them and now at least they could move on. Feeling better, she made her way back to the table where her mother was examining her face in her compact mirror.

'Where's Dad and Seb?' Lucinda asked.

'They've gone to the bar.'

'Why didn't they ask the waiter?'

Abigail shrugged and carried on admiring her reflection.

'What do you think of Seb?' Lucinda asked gingerly.

'He seems a bit wrapped up in his son,' Abigail said nastily.

'He mentioned him once,' Lucinda replied, exasperated. 'Please, Mum, what do you really think? This is important to me.'

With an angry snap Abigail shut the powder compact. 'Oh, come on, Lucinda, you're not serious. He may be a perfectly nice man but he's got a child, for heaven's sake. You're hardly stepmother material. He's probably just testing his wings after his divorce. It's just a fling, I can tell he's not serious about you.'

'But how?' Lucinda asked.

'I just can, that's all.' Her tone softened somewhat and she reached over and patted Lucinda's hand, which Lucinda thought was probably the tenderest thing she had done to her in years. 'Don't go reading too much into it, you'll only get hurt.'

Seb and her father returned, minus drinks.

'I thought you went to the bar?' Lucinda asked in a falsely cheerful voice.

'I just settled the bill. I didn't realise the time. We'd better be off if we want to catch that flight.' He looked tense and Lucinda, with a sinking feeling, realised what a terrible time he'd probably had. It was hardly the most pleasant end to a perfect weekend after all.

They said their goodbyes and, slipping into the taxi, Lucinda let out a huge sigh of relief as they drove off.

'I told you they were awful,' she said after a few moments, trying to lighten the mood.

Seb didn't say anything for a moment. His face was lined
with tension and suddenly he looked tired. 'They love you,
Lucinda,' he said finally. 'They just want what's best for
you.' But his voice was pensive instead of reassuring and
his words did nothing to comfort her.

As the plane touched down somewhat bumpily in
Melbourne, Lucinda reflected that the flight had only been
marginally less turbulent than her emotions. Seb, though
kind and pleasant, seemed lost in his thoughts and Lucinda
could almost feel him slipping away from her. It was as if
everything good had been left at the Plaza and now it was
back to the real world.

Stepping off the plane and into the arrival lounge, the air
of tension was broken by the unexpected sight of Billy and
Isabella.

'G'day, sport, this is a surprise.' Swinging him up in his
arms, Seb listened attentively as Billy chattered excitedly.

'We watched your plane land. I saw it come right along
the runway and up to the window. I could see the captain
and everything. Can I watch the bags be unloaded?'

'OK, but don't go wandering.' Seb waited until Billy was
safely out of earshot. His little face was pushed up against
the glass, watching as the ground staff unloaded the bags.
'What happened this time?' he said wearily to Isabella.

'For once she had a genuine excuse, Seb,' Isabella said
in a placating voice. 'Gemma's mum has had a fall and
probably fractured her hip. She had to fly back, of course.
It was pointless ringing you as you were probably on your
way, so I met her at the airport. You only just missed her.'

'Is she all right, apart from the hip, I mean? No other
injuries?' His voice was concerned.

'I think it's just her hip.'

'I'm sorry, Bell, you always seem to be bailing us out.'

Isabella gave her brother a friendly smile. 'I don't mind a bit. I wanted to see Billy anyway after the scare he gave us last week. But I do have to rush off. By the time I get home it will be late and I need to sort out the kids' uniforms and everything for tomorrow—they're still sitting in the laundry basket. And the kids haven't even started their homework. Dave's useless, he's probably playing footy with them in the garden as we speak.'

Seb laughed. 'Probably. Look, thanks, Bell.' Isabella made her way over to Billy to say goodbye.

'You've got to cover for Chris King,' Lucinda said.

'I know. I'll just have to take Billy in with me, I guess. Hopefully it will be quiet.'

'You can't do that,' Lucinda reasoned. 'What if there's an emergency? Look, why don't I take him back to my flat? I know Billy and he knows me. I'm sure he'd be all right about it.'

Seb didn't look too keen. 'Go on,' Lucinda insisted. 'It will be fine. You really can't take him and you can't let Chris down.'

Seb eventually agreed, and although Lucinda could tell he was reluctant she was grateful for the chance to extend the weekend and hopefully end it on a somewhat happier note. Maybe he had only agreed for her to look after Billy because he didn't have any other choice, but Lucinda was determined that this twist of fate would be the chance she wanted to show him how things could work out for them. Her mother's cruel words rang in her ears. 'Hardly stepmother material.' Well, she'd show them!

And Billy, despite his father's apparent hesitation, was delighted at the prospect of an evening with Lucinda.

'Now, you've got all your pumps?' Seb asked as he checked Billy's backpack. 'He needs the Becloforte at eight, and if there's any sign of a wheeze he's to have two puffs of the Ventolin, the blue one.'

'Seb.' Lucinda put her hand over his as he held up the pump. 'I prescribed it—remember?'

Seb looked sheepish. 'I know, and I know you can manage an asthma attack. It's just…'

'That you're his dad,' she finished the sentence for him. 'Go on, we'll be fine.'

At the car park they said their farewells and Billy climbed into the car with hardly a backward glance.

'Shouldn't you be in the back?' she asked.

'Dad always lets me go in the front,' he said.

Lucinda gave him a questioning look. 'Always?'

Billy gave a small shrug. 'Sometimes,' he admitted reluctantly.

'Well, I'd rather you sat in the back.'

Lucinda waited for an argument but Billy accepted her decision with a happy 'OK'. And he clambered into the back, clipping in his seat belt without prompting. 'Can we stop at the video shop?'

'I don't know where it is,' Lucinda replied honestly, grinning to herself at Billy's incredulous look in the rear-view mirror. 'Anyway, you can have lots of fun without watching a video.'

To Billy's remarks of 'cool' and 'what's this for?' as he wandered around her apartment, Lucinda rummaged through her hallway cupboard.

'Is that a present for me?' he asked excitedly as she brought out a huge wrapped parcel.

'It was actually for my godson,' Lucinda answered truthfully as he tore at the paper, 'but I can get him something else for Christmas.' It was probably just as well, she reflected. The wooden bagatelle set she had seen in a craft shop had evoked memories of the 'den' at boarding school where she had whiled away many an evening playing bag-atelle. Children seemed so much more advanced now. Her godson was into computers and the like. A bagatelle board probably wasn't the best gift idea she'd had.

But Billy loved it. The silver ballbearings raced around the board and they laughed and laughed as Lucinda showed him the tricks she had learnt of old. And Billy with a child's enthusiasm clasped his hands in a victory salute when finally he beat her.

Lucinda, stopping to put on the overhead light, suddenly noticed the time.

'Come on, Billy, it's time for your puffers. Do you want something to eat?' Her fridge contents didn't hold much attraction for a five-year-old so she made Vegemite on toast and poured two long glasses of orange juice.

'What did you and Dad do in Queensland?' he asked as they settled on the sofa to eat.

'We were at a medical conference.'

'Boring,' declared Billy.

'Probably to you. I saw my parents today, though. They live in Queensland.'

Billy took a bite of his toast. 'My mum lives in Sydney,' he said, without swallowing what he had eaten. 'She didn't want me to live with her.'

'But your dad did,' Lucinda replied.

'I heard Mum say once I was an accident.'

Lucinda took a swig of her juice. Billy, she decided, was playing to his audience and, awful as the truth was, she wasn't going to give him the satisfaction of a shocked look. 'So was I.'

It was Billy who looked shocked. 'Really? How did you know?'

'Same as you. I heard my mum tell someone.' Billy seemed pleased with this information, and they chatted a while. He really was the cutest kid. Terribly spoilt, Lucinda decided, probably from Seb trying to overcompensate and a multitude of nurses won over by that smile, but there was also a really great person there, a fun little man who was kind and good and clever, not unlike his father. The evening they'd spent had, in fact, Lucinda thought as she tucked a blanket round him, been probably one of the best she'd ever had. It had certainly been the funniest.

Once Billy was asleep she rang Surayan's and ordered a curry. It had been ages since she and Seb had shared that first night together. It was a calculated move and she knew it. A happy, contented child asleep, a gorgeous meal—all that was left was for her to put on some make-up and Seb would realise what a great mum she could be.

Her plans were to no avail, though. The intercom buzzed and she had time only to run a quick comb through her hair.

'You're back already?'

Seb gave a small smile. 'Chris said the wedding was awful and he was glad of the excuse to get away. Still, he was there long enough to hear about your lecture.'

'My lecture? But how?'

'News has filtered back that a star is born. Apparently Professor Hays, buoyed by a couple of glasses of champagne, is walking around singing your praises. How's Billy been?'

Lucinda gestured to the sleeping child. 'He's been fine, we had a great night. He fell asleep about fifteen minutes ago. He had all his pumps,' she said before Seb had a chance to ask. 'Any news at the hospital? How's Kimberley?'

Seb shook his head. 'Not good, I'm afraid. I didn't see her but apparently there's an NFR order.'

Lucinda turned away and busied herself, wiping the

bench, so that Seb couldn't see her face. Hastily she wiped away a tear. An NFR order meant 'not for resuscitation'. For Janine and Mark to have agreed to that, it must mean there was no hope. It was awful news, and by now she should be used to it, but...

'Anything else?' she asked in a strangely high voice.

'I met up with Vince Cole on his way home—he'd been in with a patient. We had a long chat about Billy and his asthma—he's quite good at straight talking.'

Her composure restored, Lucinda turned and made her way over to him.

'Speaking of straight talking, Seb, is something wrong? We've hardly exchanged a word since we left my parents.'

He ran a hand through his hair and Lucinda felt her heart plummet as his eyes avoided hers.

'I've been doing some thinking.' He paused and Lucinda knew what was coming. 'There's something worrying me, I just don't know how to say it.'

She swallowed hard. Her mother had been right after all, it had all just been a fling. Longing for him to put her mind at rest, to somehow reassure her that she was mistaken, her heart sank further as he tentatively continued struggling with his words.

'We really need to talk. I just don't see how this is going to work. You've got so much going for you, I just can't imagine...' Seb's voice trailed off and finally he gestured to Billy, asleep on the sofa.

'It's just that I can't... You're not...'

Lucinda finished the sentence for him. 'Not stepmum material.'

'I didn't say that,' he said fiercely.

As the world crashed around her, the Lucinda who was good at hiding her feelings, of staying in control, came to the fore. Somehow she managed a smile, determined to escape with some dignity. If Seb wanted to end things, she damn well wasn't going to let him think it was solely his decision. She had some pride. 'You didn't have to. I'd actually started to realise that myself.'

Seb looked at her, his eyes full of confusion. 'You had?'

'Having him here tonight. I mean, we had fun and everything, but…well, look, you're right. I don't see how it could work. It's just not for me. It's no big deal. We're consenting adults after all. We had a good time, no one got hurt, we can still be friends.'

Seb gave a small nod. 'Of course.'

He made his way over to Billy who stirred gently as Seb lifted him. The love in his eyes when he gazed at his son made her want to weep. She was so sure she had seen it there before, but for her.

'Hold on a moment,' she called as he made his way to the lift. Grabbing a bag, she stuffed the bagatelle set into it. 'I said he could have it.'

'You don't have to, Lucinda.'

'Please.' She gave a small laugh. 'What am I going to do with it?'

She stood there watching the numbers go down on the lift lights, watching as the two males she loved walk out of her life. She was still standing there when the lift returned and Vijay's son arrived with the curry. Somehow she paid him and chatted about the weather. Somehow she made it back into her apartment.

Numb, shocked, she made her way into the shower, standing quite still until eventually the water ran cold. And even then she didn't notice. 'No one got hurt,' she'd said. That had been the biggest lie of her life, for the pain that she was feeling now was utterly indescribable. Finally, shivering, she made her way to bed, the curry having long since gone cold. There she lay alone and waited for morning.

Monday was easily the blackest day of Lucinda's life. Somehow she had thought to set the alarm and had awoken to the smell of cold curry and the painful memories of the previous night. It seemed impossible to believe that only twenty-four hours ago she had woken in Seb's arms and made love. How, she wrestled with herself, could she have been so wrong? How could she have misread him so badly? 'A fling', her mother had said, and she had been right, it seemed.

The ward round was painfully slow and when they finally walked into NICU the sight of Janine and Mark at Kimberley's incubator was almost too much to take.

'How's Kimberley?' Lucinda asked Andrew Doran.

He shook his head. 'Her parents want another CT scan, but it's pointless.'

'Will you do one?'

Andrew nodded. 'I think it's merited if it helps Janine and Mark. She's going down soon.'

Making her way across to the catheter suite, Lucinda checked the whiteboard. Seb was the anaesthetist on. Bracing herself, she walked in, only to find Chris King checking his equipment.

'Good morning, Lucinda, or should I say good afternoon?'

Lucinda managed a cheery greeting as Chris explained he was filling in for Seb who was stuck on the wards. His excuse was plausible enough but Lucinda felt it was rather more convenient than facing her today of all days.

They were busy for the next few hours and Lucinda was more than happy to concentrate on others' hearts. Her own was in a mess.

When the last of the patients had been dealt with, she made her way to the canteen. Lunch orders had finished so there were only sandwiches available from the machine. The canteen was relatively quiet but, longing for some peace, she made her way up to her office. As she reached the top of the stairwell she was met by the grief-stricken faces of Janine and Mark.

'Has Kimberley gone for her scan?' she asked, full of concern.

Mark shook his head and pulled the sobbing Janine towards him.

'We decided not to send her, she'd been through enough. Seb came and extubated her. She died soon after...' His voice broke. 'We were both holding her.'

Lucinda stood there, frozen. She had seen raw grief so many—too many—times, but it was something she knew she would never get used to. 'I'm so very sorry,' she said, her voice thick with emotion.

'We're just going to the hospital chapel and then we're going to go back and spend some time with her.'

Lucinda nodded.

Janine looked up and Lucinda couldn't bear to see the pain in her eyes.

'Thank you for all you did. Everyone's been wonderful.'

'I just wish we could have done more.'

Mark shook her hand and guided his wife gently towards the chapel. Numb, Lucinda walked the few steps to her office. Taking off her white coat, she sat at her desk and stared at her hands for a few moments. Then the tears came, rolling out of her eyes, splashing onto her hands, and she did nothing to stop them. It took a moment or two before she realised someone was knocking on her door.

'One moment.' Hastily she wiped her tears away and blew her nose. 'Come in.'

It was Seb. 'Sorry to disturb you.'

'No problem.' She forced a smile.

'I didn't want you to think I was avoiding you this morning, not that it would be possible in a place like this even if I wanted to, which I don't.'

'Like I said, we're adults. It's not as if we were married or anything. We can all make mistakes.'

'You've been crying?'

She was about to deny it, but what was the point? Her face was probably bright red. 'I just saw Janine and Mark Stewart.'

'It's awful, isn't it? That's where I've been. I've had a fair bit to do with them over the last couple of months and I wanted to see things through.'

Which was so like him, Lucinda thought, taking the hard road when he didn't have to, giving that bit more. She could read the concern for her in his eyes, and she knew if she started to cry again she wouldn't be able to stop. She couldn't let him see her like that. They had made a deal. Friends, remember?

'You had a bit to do with Janine. Is that why this one's hit you so hard?' Seb asked gently.

How could she tell him? Yesterday maybe, but yesterday they had been a couple. Today he was a colleague. How could she tell him that they all hit her like this? That the name of each child that had died was etched on her heart? That right now she would love to grab her bag and run? Put as much distance as she could from this place and never come back? Instead, she gave a tight smile, the persona of cool.

'That must be it. She seemed like a nice woman. It was to be expected, of course. Twenty-four weeks is barely viable and Kimberley had a lot of problems besides immaturity.' She picked up a file and reached for her Dictaphone. Miss Chambers was back!

But Seb seemed to see through her bravado. 'Lucinda, are you sure you're all right?'

She longed to tell him she wasn't, that Kimberley's death, him leaving, they had both devastated her, but instead her face remained impassive. 'Of course. I'm fine. It's sad and all that but, well, it comes with the job.' And clicking on her Dictaphone, she opened the file in front of her and flashed Seb a cool smile. 'I'll catch up with you later. I really am snowed under.'

Seb raised his eyebrows at her reaction, but didn't comment. Without another word he turned and left, closing the door behind him. She heard his footsteps fading down the corridor and only when she was safely alone did she put her head down on the desk and weep. She wept for them all—for Kimberley and Janine and Mark and then for herself. In a few short hours everything had changed and life for them all would never be the same again.

CHAPTER EIGHT

As Seb had pointed out, if they had wanted to avoid each other they couldn't, and in the weeks that followed they were thrown together often.

Lucinda coped by day. They had polite conversations when she asked about Billy and he asked about her work, but it wasn't enough. From answering 'better' and 'fine' to her questions his answers had become 'not bad' and 'getting there'. She had heard from her peers that Billy's asthma was worsening and she yearned for more information and deep down she ached to see him for herself.

At least workwise things had never been better. November turned into December and the operation lists were overflowing as they tried to get the numbers down before scheduled operations ceased over Christmas. It was a blessing in disguise as the days flew by and Lucinda could bury herself in work and forget about her own problems.

It was a different question at night, though. Exhausted, she would collapse on the sofa. Not even hungry, she would have a couple of slices of toast or a biscuit if there were any, before collapsing on the bed. There she would lie and wait for sleep, trying to block all thoughts of Seb out of her mind, determined not to cry herself to sleep again. But eventually the tears would win and she would awake puffy-eyed and tired, only to start another weary day all over again.

Sitting at her desk one morning, she dunked a teabag in a cup of hot water and decided to tackle the mountain of internal mail that had piled up. Most were Christmas cards, and she made a mental note to stop at the shops on the way home and buy a couple more boxes. Everywhere in the hospital was decorated with tinsel and flashing lights. The children's ward was abuzz with excitement and nurses walked around with flashing Christmas-tree earrings.

Lucinda, at Ann's insistence, had stuck a piece of tinsel around her name badge but that was as far as her festive preparations went. It seemed like a lifetime since she had been happy but it had, in fact, only been eight weeks. Eight weeks of hell. She felt like she had forgotten how to smile naturally and could hear herself barking at the staff. So much for festive cheer. She was living right up to her reputation and decided to try and brighten up.

It was to no avail, though, for as she opened a yellow envelope a memo greeted her, and as she read the words about the recent resignation of Dr Carlisle, it was as if a knife were being plunged straight into her heart. She sat there, trying to make sense of the words blurring before her, but before she had time to digest the contents her emergency page went off and she rushed across to CGU.

'What's the story?'

The little girl sitting on the bed, was struggling with her breathing.

Jack Wells gave her a worried look. 'Pre-op for removal of a cyst on the right lung. She's developed sudden onset of shortness of breath, with reduced air sounds on the right.'

'Has she had an X-ray?'

Jack handed the films to her. 'We just got them back after I put the page out. She's got a tension pneumothorax.'

Lucinda had a brief look at the films, confirming Jack's diagnosis.

'Ann set up for a chest drain. Put her oxygen up, Jack, to one hundred per cent. What's her sats?'

Jack checked the saturation machine.

'Ninety per cent on one hundred per cent oxygen.'

'OK. Let's put a tube in now. Right, Jack, you can do this one.'

She saw the anxiety on his face and she knew he was nervous, but he had done this procedure before, albeit not in an emergency.

'Come on, Jack, you can do this.' She watched his trembling hands.

'That's right—between fourth and fifth intercostal spaces. Now inject your local.'

Ellen spoke to the young girl who was concentrating too hard on her breathing to be scared, while Ann assisted the doctors.

'Now push till you feel it give. That's it—further. You're in. OK, now remove the guide.' The bottle by the bed connected to the chest tube bubbled merrily with each breath. 'Now stitch the chest tube firmly in place.' She listened to the girl's chest. 'Much better. Good air entry. When you've finished stitching her she'll need a repeat chest X-ray.'

Lucinda watched closely as Jack, his confidence up now, deftly stitched the tube in place. The ward was very warm and Lucinda felt the beads of sweat rising on her forehead and trickling between her breasts. Suddenly she felt quite dizzy. 'All right, Jack, you carry on from here.' With the ward spinning, she made her way to the office and sat on the nearest chair, taking some deep breaths. Serve her right for skipping breakfast and lunch, too, for that matter. She really had to start taking better care of herself. Ann came in quietly and closed the door.

'Are you all right, Lucinda?'

'Just felt a bit hot in there. The air-conditioning in this place leaves a lot to be desired.

'When did you last eat?'

Lucinda gave a small shrug.

'Yesterday, I think.'

Ann tutted loudly. 'I actually saved you some mince pies.' She pushed the plate toward her. Lucinda took a look at the curling pastry and shook her head.

'A rum ball, then?'

Lucinda gave her a smile. 'I'm fine, Ann, really. I think I'll grab some sandwiches from the machine.'

'How about some cornflakes? We've got some on the ward. Save you going down to the canteen.'

'I guess I did miss breakfast—that sounds good.'

Ann scuttled off and returned a few moments later with two small boxes and a carton of milk. She set about preparing them and poured on some sugar.

Lucinda tucked in, realising how hungry she was.

Ann hovered, ensuring Lucinda cleared the bowl. 'You certainly enjoyed them,' she said cheerfully, then her tone changed and Lucinda listened as she continued in a searching voice. 'Cornflakes were all I could manage myself when I was pregnant.' And Lucinda knew Ann's words had been carefully chosen. With a clatter Lucinda dropped the spoon back into the bowl and stared at the empty plate, not saying a word.

'Didn't you realise?' Ann asked gently.

Lucinda sat for a while before answering. 'Not really,' she replied quietly.

Ann, bless her, didn't bat an eyelid. 'So you haven't done a test yet?'

Lucinda shook her head, trying to blink back tears.

'I take it this isn't a planned pregnancy.'

It was all Lucinda could do to shake her head.

'I'm sure you're worrying about nothing, it could be a false alarm.'

Lucinda gave a hollow laugh. 'I don't need to do a test.

I've had it at the back of my mind for the last few weeks. I guess I was trying to avoid facing up to it.'

'Ignoring it won't make it go away.'

'How did you guess?' Lucinda asked. 'Is it that obvious?'

'Only to me. I had terrible morning sickness with my boys, couldn't eat a thing. For someone like you who loves their tucker to suddenly be eating like a sparrow, well, I had a good inkling. Then seeing you go faint when Jack put in the chest drain. Cardiothoracic surgeons don't normally have weak stomachs. It all added up. Do you want to talk about it, Lucinda, or do you want me to mind my own business?'

Lucinda thought for a moment. Ann was the one person she knew who wouldn't be remotely offended if she told her to butt out. But she needed to talk, she needed some help badly.

'You don't mind me dumping this on you?'

Ann gave a big smile. 'See these shoulders? They're wide for a reason. Now, you take this.' She rummaged in her drawer and pulled out a specimen bottle. 'I don't need to tell you what to do with this. I'll pop over to the gynae ward and grab a pregnancy test. I'll have a check on the ward as well and then I'll tell Ellen we don't want to be disturbed. She'll just think we're going over a patient or the budget or something.'

Lucinda nodded. 'Ann,' she called to her departing back.

The woman swung around. 'You don't have to say it—I won't breathe a word.'

Lucinda shook her head. 'I know that already. I was going to say thanks for being here, for helping.'

Ann came over and gave her a warm hug. 'I haven't started yet.'

Waiting for Ann to return, Lucinda paced the floor. How,

she tried to fathom, could she have let this happen? Of all the stupid mistakes to make. She was a doctor and so was Seb for that matter. They should both have known better. But that beautiful Sunday morning as she had lain so warm in bed next to him, had felt his male urges stirring, their bodies awakening together, consequences and ramifications had seemed a million miles away. Even at the memory of his touch she felt a stirring within. It had all seemed so right then. She'd thought they'd had all the time in the world. How could she have known that it had all been about to end, barely before it had started?

Ann returned, putting the 'Knock and Wait' sign on the door.

'Are you ready?' she asked as she unwrapped the package which would determine her fate.

Lucinda shook her head. 'No, but do it anyway.'

Those two minutes were probably the longest of her life. She thought of the niggling worry, pushed to the back of her mind over the past few weeks, growing as the days passed and her symptoms became more apparent. At first she had put the exhaustion down to stress, lack of sleep, and they were both good reasons. Since Seb had gone from her life she felt as if she were living two lives, by day the consummate professional but by night a child lost. The nausea she had blamed on gastro, a bad take-away—anything but this. Lucinda wasn't a woman who wrote her cycles in her diary, like she never filled out her cheque stubs, so she'd had no idea when she'd been due. But as the weeks had dragged on and nothing had happened, she had known her fears were with good foundation and now she was about to have it confirmed. The result was a foregone conclusion.

Ann glanced at the indicator. 'Well, I don't think that leaves any room for doubt.' She pushed the test over the desk and Lucinda stared at the dark pink cross that had formed on the blotting paper. It felt strange. Nothing had changed from two minutes ago—she was still a doctor a woman—yet *everything* had changed. She was now pregnant. Growing inside her was a baby, a person in its own right, a permanent legacy of when her life had been perfect.

'Oh, God,' she groaned. 'Ann what am I going to do?'

Ann was over in a flash. 'You'll be fine,' she reassured. 'You'll do whatever has to be done. I take it this isn't the news you were hoping for?'

Lucinda shook her head.

'Then you're going to have to make some decisions.'

Lucinda stared at the pregnancy test for a moment and then looked up at Ann.

'I can't end the pregnancy, Ann, it just isn't me.'

Ann gave her a smile. 'Well, as strange as it might seem, I'm going to say it anyway—congratulations, Lucinda. It might not feel it now but this is going to be the best thing that's ever happened to you, and you hold on to that thought through all the difficult times. When you hold your baby in your arms all the problems you've had getting there will seem minute, I promise you that.' She gave her a hug.

'Do you want to tell me who the father is?'

Lucinda thought for a moment and took a deep breath. 'Seb,' she said quietly.

Again Ann managed not to look remotely surprised. 'I thought that was the way the wind was blowing for a while, and then it all seemed to die down. I'm glad I'm not losing my touch.'

Lucinda managed a small smile.

'Seb's a wonderful man,' Ann enthused. 'He'll be delighted. He'll take care of you.'

Lucinda angrily wiped away a tell-tale tear that had escaped down her cheek. 'It's not that straightforward. He's already had one failed marriage, remember. He's not going in to bat again unless the pitch is perfect—he said as much.'

'Maybe this will give him the push he needs. I'm an expert where Seb's concerned. Seb would never have slept with you if he wasn't serious. That man has had loads of women after him before, during and after his marriage, and he's never looked twice. He would never have let things get this far if he didn't think you were pretty special.'

'I think he does love me in some way, but there's Billy to consider. He doesn't think I'm stepmum material, he said so.'

'Seb said that?' Ann exclaimed, this time failing to keep the shock from her voice. 'I can't believe that—are you sure?'

'I was there, remember. He doesn't think I'm up to the job of being a stepmother. What on earth's he going to say when he finds out I'm actually having his baby? What if he's right? What if I'm not up to it.'

'Now, we'll have none of that talk,' Ann said firmly. 'Lucinda, you'll be a wonderful mother—don't you ever doubt that. And when Seb hears I'm sure, once the shock wears off, he'll be delighted, too.'

'I'm not going to tell him.' Lucinda said firmly.

Ann stood up. 'Lucinda I know I'm a mere nurse and you're the one with the medical degree but, without meaning to state the obvious, it's going to become pretty clear to everyone that you're pregnant. You said yourself that you're going to keep the baby and you're hardly going to leave work now and get a new job. Seb's going to have to be told.'

'No, he isn't.' With a shaking hand she retrieved the screwed-up memo from her pocket and handed it to Ann, who read it silently. 'He's handed in his notice,' Lucinda said wearily 'He's taking up a Chief of Anaesthetics position in Ballarat. He's leaving next month.'

'But he'll still hear about the baby—you know how word spreads.'

'By the time he hears he'll just assume I've met someone else.'

'Lucinda, he has a right to know,' Ann said, exasperated.

'No, Ann,' Lucinda said firmly 'He had a right when we were together. I'm not going to go to him with a begging bowl for a few dollars and some access visits I'd rather manage on my own. And, please, Ann, promise not to breathe a word.'

Ann nodded. 'You don't have to worry about that, it's not my place to tell him.' She sat down again. 'Right, let's deal with the practicalities. Have you managed to find a GP since you moved here?'

'No, there's been no need till now.'

'Right, I'll ring mine for you. I'll do it now. She's ever so good. Is that all right?'

Lucinda nodded her consent as Ann made the call.

'She can fit you in at two o'clock tomorrow—can you get away?'

Lucinda nodded her agreement. She had to get seen after all. This was going to be the first of many doctors' visits her schedule would have to accommodate.

'Ann, I haven't taken folate or been sleeping or eating properly. What if I've done the baby some harm?'

'Well, considering the way you ate before you got pregnant one could safely assume that you've got enough iron stores to open a mine, but welcome to motherhood.' Ann smiled. 'You never stop worrying.'

'How are you feeling?' Ann gave Lucinda a smile as she walked on the ward for the Christmas party.

'Terrified. It's a bit like getting ready for a date. I've spent an hour in the shower, shaved my legs, checked my bag a million times.'

'What for?' Ann laughed.

'Clean underpants, specimen jar, medicare card, private health cover card.'

'You wait till the baby gets here, you'll need a juggernaut to carry your bag then.'

Everyone gathered around the tree. Past patients and their parents, doctors, nurses. All the children's beds and cots had been moved and formed a huge arc around the tree, and the children's faces were expectant. Lucinda concentrated on the tree, trying not to catch Seb's eye as he held for dear life onto a thoroughly over-excited Billy.

Ann stepped forward. 'Now, we all know Christmas is a few days off but for very special children, which you all are, special things happen so Father Christmas has taken some time out of his busy schedule to pay you all a visit.' She put her hands up to her ears as the sound of bells filled the corridor.

'What's that noise?' she asked the grinning faces.

The children cheered and even the most unwell managed to sit up in their beds.

'*Ho! Ho! Ho!*' The doors swung open and Professor Hays, hardly needing any stuffing in his outfit, burst in as the place erupted. The next twenty minutes were mayhem as the children gathered round, extracting their gifts, all painstakingly chosen by Ann and beautifully wrapped. And finally when each child had opened their present and were chewing on the surprises in their lolly bags or tucking into cherries and mandarins if they were diabetic, the carols started.

Lucinda joined in with 'We Wish You A Merry Christmas', but as the cassette started to play 'Away In a

Manger' and the little voices joined in, it was too much. Stealing a look around the ward at the little faces covered by oxygen masks, the drips and monitors, she felt a huge lump in her throat. As happy as the ward was, it was tinged with sadness because they all knew for some it would be their last Christmas, and she thought of the ones like baby Kimberley who never even got to see one. Quietly she slipped away to the privacy of Ann's office. She wasn't alone. Ann had beaten her to it, sitting at her desk, with shaking shoulders.

'That hymn gets me every time,' she said with great tears pouring down her face as Lucinda entered.

Lucinda managed a smile, determined not to break down in front of anyone. 'I'll get you a tissue.'

'There aren't any—the kids all used them to have a snowball fight this morning,' Ann said through her tears, and as she held up a toilet roll it reminded Lucinda so much of that morning with Billy that there was nothing else to do but have a good cry.

With a sob she took the roll from Ann and tore off a few sheets. 'At least I can blame it on my hormones.'

Neither heard at first as Seb and Billy entered.

'Sorry to barge in, but Billy wanted to see you both,' Seb explained, his gaze not quite reaching Lucinda's eyes.

Billy handed them both a small parcel and Lucinda opened hers somewhat shakily.

A tiny gold robot stared back at her, and she swallowed hard a couple of times as she looked at it.

'Thank you, Billy, it's beautiful.' Ann had the same.

'It's to go on your necklace, I bought it with my own pocket money. They're solid gold,' Billy said importantly.

'Solid gold-*coloured*, Billy. You can't be too careful in these days of litigation. Billy managed to find a robot tie-

pin for Professor Hays, which I know he's going to love.'
Seb gave the women a wink.

'We can't find him anywhere, but guess what?'

'What's that?' Lucinda asked.

'I think the professor looks a bit like Father Christmas.
Dad said it's because they're both magic.'

'Notice anything different about me?' a theatrical voice
boomed from the open door. Bianca stood there with a huge
smile.

'Your braces are gone!' Lucinda exclaimed.

'Yes, yes,' Bianca said dismissively. 'But there's something else, can't you see?'

They all stared for a moment as Bianca stood there impatiently waiting. 'I'm wearing a bra!'

'So you are, and don't you look just gorgeous?' Ann
exclaimed.

Seb managed a small blush. 'Well, we'll leave you ladies
to discuss your secret women's business.' He laughed. 'Say
goodbye and thank you, Billy.'

As they left the office it took every ounce of self-control
she could muster to stop herself from running after the two
most important people in her life. Instead, she clung onto
the tiny metallic robot as Bianca handed Ann a present and
spoke at length about her recent growth spurt.

'I got something for you, too.'

'For me? How lovely you didn't need to do that.'
Lucinda opened the parcel to reveal the video of the film
they had been watching the night Bianca had arrested.

Lucinda was touched and told her so.

'See, you said there'd be a happy ending, and here I am.'
She gave Lucinda and Ann a small thumbs-up.

Lucinda gave Bianca a hug. 'That's true, but since that
night I've never been able to eat pizza.'

Bianca gave a laugh. 'Actually, neither have I.'

Once they were alone again, the room fell silent.

'This will be my last Christmas here. I think it's time to hang up my apron,' Ann said suddenly.

Lucinda looked at her, aghast. 'You can't be serious. This place would collapse without you.'

'No, it wouldn't, it would manage just fine. It gets harder each year, thinking about all the ones we've lost. I'm thinking of getting a nice job in a nursing home. At least when someone dies there you know they've had a fair crack.'

Lucinda thought for a moment. 'But you seem to cope so well with it all.'

'"Seem to" is right. It takes its toll on all of us, Lucinda, even you, I'm sure.'

Lucinda gave a small shrug. If she confided this to Ann she knew she would be lost. 'I just look at the bigger picture. Look at Billy, look at Bianca—there's more wins than losses.'

Ann gave her a quizzical look. 'Well, the wins are great but the losses are just too hard to take sometimes. You'd better go if you want to make your appointment.'

Lucinda made her way out of the hospital and took a tram to the address Ann had given her. She had been tempted to confide in Ann about her own feelings about work, too, but what good would it do? Even if she wanted to she couldn't leave now; she was hardly in the position for a career change. She was going to need her salary now more than ever.

CHAPTER NINE

DR INNES went over to the sink and washed her hands as Lucinda stood up and got dressed.

The GP got out a daisy wheel and started fiddling with it.

'So you don't know the date of your last menstrual period?'

'Er, no, but my dates are definitely right. You see, it could only have been then.'

Dr Innes gave her a small smile and reached for a pad.

'I think we might arrange for an ultrasound. Mr Field is an excellent obstetrician and he does his own ultrasounds. He's very nice to talk to, especially for first-time mums. I know you're a doctor but you'll still have a lot of questions.'

'I thought you didn't do routine scans until eighteen weeks. Is there a problem?'

Dr Innes hesitated for a moment. 'There's no problem, but your uterus seems rather larger than I'd expect at this stage, and if you're sure about your dates...' She carried on writing.

Lucinda felt as if the chair had been whipped from beneath her. She'd already had enough shocks in the last twenty-four hours, but now this! Her voice came out in an unsteady rasp. 'You're not thinking it could be twins?'

'Let's just wait and see, shall we?'

How many times had she herself said that to an anxious mother when she'd organised a test? But sitting on the other side of the fence, well, it was a whole new experience. 'How long till he'll be able to see me?'

Dr Innes reached for her phone. 'He's very popular but I know him well and, with you being a doctor, I'll see what I can do. I'm sure he'll squeeze you in. I must admit I'd want to know myself.'

Twins. Twins! It didn't bear thinking about. How on earth was she going to tell Seb this? And her mother!

'He'll see you in half an hour. Have you been to the loo recently?'

Lucinda shook her head.

'Good.' She went over to the sink and filled a glass with water. 'Drink this—all of it—so he gets a good view. I expect you need a glass of water anyway. It might be a false alarm. It will be nice to have a scan anyway. Sometimes it helps you get used to the idea of being pregnant if it wasn't planned.'

Bursting for the loo, she waited anxiously in the waiting room, trying and failing not to think about the impossibilities of raising two children. So much for her career. Single parents didn't make the best cardiothoracic consultants or so she thought. It wasn't as if she could think of one who had tried, but as a single parent of twins, it seemed impossible.

'Miss Chambers?' Expecting to see the receptionist, Lucinda reached for her bag and stood up.

'Just coming.' She was stunned when she saw the smiling face of Janine Stewart.

'I bet you weren't expecting to see me here. Are you here to review a patient?'

Lucinda gave a noncommittal shrug. 'Something like that. How are you, Janine? How are you and Mark coping?'

'It's been awful,' she admitted honestly. 'It still is. I expect it's going to take a long time. We've both been walk-

ing around like a couple of zombies, we just miss her
so.' She wiped away a tear with the back of her hand.
'Christmas is going to be hard but, then, every day is. Mark
was worried about me so he took me back for a check-up,
and guess what?'

Lucinda didn't know what to say. They were in an obstetrician's waiting room after all, but what if she was
wrong? Maybe they were here to give IVF another go.

'It's all right,' Janine said. 'We can't believe it either,
but I really am. The one time in ten years we're not trying
for a baby I go and get pregnant. The doctors don't know
what to make of it, but I am having a baby, and it's all
down to you.'

'Me? But how?'

'That ''competition'' you pretended to win. I don't know
what they put in the curry but it worked. We only did it
the once. Still, I guess that's all it takes.'

Lucinda gave Janine a wide smile. 'That's fantastic, but
how are you coping with it, after all you've been through?'

'I'm trying not to get my hopes up, but I've just got a
feeling it's meant to be. I even *feel* pregnant this time. With
Kimberley I never did. Mr Field says I'm pumping with
hormones and it all looks great on the ultrasound. After all
the emotion of the past few weeks and me not knowing, I
haven't been making allowances. Well, the fact I'm still
pregnant is amazing in itself. In some ways I didn't want
to be if that makes any sense. I felt this baby was sort of
intruding on my grief for Kimberley, but I'm getting there.'

'It's a lot for you to deal with, but it's the most fantastic
news. Where's Mark? He must be thrilled.'

'He's the same as me, just taking it one day at a time.
But we're together and we're happy so we've got a lot to
be grateful for, whatever happens.' A car tooted noisily
outside, 'That will be Mark, we couldn't get a parking

space nearer. Look, I won't be coming back to the Women's and Children's with this one. Obviously, if there's a problem I'll have no choice, but we kind of wanted to go somewhere else this time—not that you weren't all fantastic,' Janine added hastily.

'I understand. I'd feel exactly the same.'

'I know you won't want to give out your address so I won't ask, but can I drop you a line at the hospital and let you know how things go?'

'Don't be silly. Here.' Lucinda scribbled her home address on a piece of paper and handed it to Janine. 'Give me yours. It will be nice to keep in touch.'

The car tooted again and Janine wrote quickly.

'Good luck,' Lucinda called as Janine went out to her husband.

'Miss Chambers.' This time there was no mistaking the summons.

Straightening her shoulders, Lucinda turned and smiled.

'Just coming,' she said, and, following the receptionist, made her way down to the ultrasound room, wondering what fate held for her.

Mr Field was, as promised, a lovely doctor, chatty but professional. He introduced himself and asked a few questions.

'Well, I won't keep you in suspense. We'll go over everything thoroughly in your first antenatal appointment. Let's find out, shall we?'

He helped her onto the examination couch and placed the blanket over her as Lucinda lifted her gown. He squirted cold jelly onto her abdomen and Lucinda lay there, rigid.

'Do you want to see the screen?'

Lucinda thought for a moment. 'Not yet.'

He placed the probe on her abdomen and pushed against her full bladder. Lucinda listened to the familiar crackling as the machine zoned in. And then she heard it, loud and regular, her baby's heartbeat.

'Well, there's definitely one in there,' Mr Field stated. 'I'll do the measurements in a minute.' He moved the probe slightly and in just a few seconds Lucinda heard the same rapid sound. 'And there's number two.'

She lay there for a moment as the news sank in. Somehow hearing the heartbeats made it all seem a bit better—it was a sound she heard every day. But these were her own babies' heartbeats she was hearing, and it really was like music to her ears. She thought of Janine who had lain here before her, desperate for a child. Though this wasn't what she herself had planned, never in a million years, Lucinda there and then accepted that this was just the way it was. Lady fate had stepped in and given her not one but two babies and now she had to deal with the situation head on. Somehow she would.

'There's not another one hiding in there?' she asked nervously.

'No, just the two,' Mr Field said cheerfully.

'Can I see now?' He turned the screen and Lucinda gazed in increasing wonder at the tiny hearts beating, scarcely able to comprehend that there were two babies tumbling inside her.

Mr Field clicked away, taking measurements. 'Two placentas so they're not identical. Of course, too early to tell the sex—will you want to know?'

Lucinda shook her head. 'I'm getting used to surprises—why spoil it?'

And then it was over. Clutching her photo, she said her goodbyes, gratefully went to the loo and paid the bill. The afternoon sun was bright after the darkness of the ultrasound room. Catching the tram, she sat by a window and fished the picture from her bag. Looking up, she saw an old woman smiling at her.

'Is that your baby?' she asked, offering Lucinda a toffee.

Lucinda took the toffee with a smile. 'Actually, I'm having twins—see.' She showed her the photo.

'Looks like a map of the moon to me, but congratulations, love. Here, you'd better have another one.' She offered Lucinda another toffee. 'You'll be needing to keep your sugar up.'

Back at the hospital, unlocking her office, she paled as she saw Seb making his way out of PICU.

'Lucinda.' He gave her a smile.

'Where's Billy?'

'There's a Christmas party on Chest Med which he "had" to go to. Little devil. He's cleaned Father Christmas out already and it isn't even the twenty-fifth.' Though he was smiling, she could see the tiredness on his face.

'You're leaving,' she said simply.

Seb nodded. 'Seems my speech went down well. John told me at the conference about this job. I was only half listening but, well, things just aren't working out here. I don't want Billy to go to boarding school and I'm sick of nannies. This job's practically nine to five. It's a promotion, I know, but leaving a hospital like this for the country, some would see it as a bit of a side step. All the same, it's what I want.'

'Is it?'

Seb stared at her for a long time. Oh, she wanted so badly to put her hand up and touch his face but she just stood there. 'Sure, it's more admin than I'd like but Billy has to come first. His asthma is getting worse, and the country air will improve it. We'll be near Bella. As she pointed out, she's got four kids already so what's another one in the school holidays? Billy will have to go to after-school care a couple of nights or to Bella's but I'll be able to take him most mornings. He'll have his dad around, and Bella can be a constant feminine role model. He needs that, Lucinda. Gemma is being good but she's not going to provide what he needs.'

And it all made perfect sense. Seb was right—he did have to go. But it didn't stop her heart from aching as she listened.

'When are you leaving?'

'Two weeks. I'm just covering over Christmas and New Year. Billy's going to spend it in Sydney with Gemma and her parents. I can finish up here and do the big move myself. I think it would be all a bit much for him otherwise. I want to get Billy settled into his new home before he starts school. We've found a house.'

'Nice?'

'Too big, but it's got stables and Billy is desperate for a horse. We've done the allergy tests and unfortunately for me that's the one thing he's not allergic to, so it's going to be up at the crack of dawn for me, mucking out stables.'

Lucinda managed a smile. The vision of Seb and Billy riding together made her want to cry. He had got his life all sorted—how could she tell him now? Surely it was better this way?

'Sounds fun,' she replied lightly, but it came out all wrong, as if she was being sarcastic. Seb gave her a strange look

'It probably sounds awful to you, but I'm kind of looking forward to it.'

She gave a nod, terrified her voice might betray her again.

'You'll come to my leaving party.'

'Of course.'

And that was it. Lucinda lingered a moment, watching

him walk smartly along the ward. How she longed to call him back, to explain her apparent indifference. But how could she? That would mean telling him about the twins. How could she ruin his life just when he had it on track? She simply couldn't do it to him and to Billy.

And so she retreated back to where she was safe. Back to the days of old before Billy and Seb had spun her life around. She smiled less and worked ever harder, if that was possible.

Christmas Eve came and the hospital was in a frenzy of excitement. Although the theatres were only open for emergencies, Lucinda was kept busy with outpatients and ward work. Finally she made her way over to CGU.

'Anything for me?'

'Of course.' Ann gave her a smile. The ward was more than half-empty. 'Robert Good is doing amazingly well.' She nodded her head to the bed where a pale young boy lay. Lucinda had performed cardiac mesh repair on him only two days previously. 'I know it's a bit soon but his parents have asked, as he's doing so well, could you consider him for day leave tomorrow? Jack had a look, but said it was your call.'

Lucinda nodded. 'Yes, he mentioned it. What do you think?'

Ann gave a small shrug. 'He seems all right but, to be honest, if it was my son who had just had cardiac surgery I wouldn't want him home yet. I tried telling the parents, but you know what some people are like. They don't think we're doing much for him and think I'm just being pedantic.'

'OK, I'll take a look.' She walked over to the young patient. 'Good afternoon, Robert. How are you feeling?'

'Great. I just want to go home.'

Lucinda gave him a smile. 'Well, let's have a look at you.'

His parents hovered anxiously, obviously keen to have their son home.

'He feels a bit warm. What was his temp?'

Ann checked the chart. 'Thirty-seven at four o'clock.'

'Could you just check it again, please?'

Ann put the tympanic thermometer into the young boy's ear.

'Thirty-seven four.'

Lucinda finished her examination.

'Could I have a word, please?' She called the parents over to the office.

'I'm not happy for Robert to have day leave,' she said.

'But why not? Is something wrong?' Mr Good asked tersely.

'He has a low-grade temperature that I'd like to keep an eye on. It's probably nothing to worry about but I'd rather he stayed here.'

Mr Good stiffened his shoulders. 'Well, if his temperature's normal tomorrow, can he go home?'

'I'd really rather he stayed.'

'What's a couple of hours?' Mr Good demanded. 'It's not as if you're doing anything for him now. Just a couple of pills here and there. The kid should be home for Christmas.'

Lucinda began to feel irritated but kept her voice even.

'Mr and Mrs Good, I explained to you in Outpatients that if the operation was done on the twenty-second it would mean your son would have to spend Christmas in hospital, to which you agreed.'

'Yes,' Mr Good admitted. 'But he's done better than expected. Surely there's room for a bit of leniency? We've bought him a new computer game and he's desperate to try it out. What's he going to do here all day?'

Lucinda stiffened. 'Here skilled nursing staff will monitor him. If he develops a temperature, bloods will be taken promptly and if, heaven forbid, he develops any of a multitude of post-operative complications there will be staff immediately on hand to deal with them. As much as I can understand your desire to have your son home for Christmas, even allowing for leniency, I cannot in good faith allow him to go.'

Mr Good huffed and puffed a bit longer but Lucinda stood firm and finally they retreated to Robert's bed.

'Well, that told them. Good for you,' Ann remarked.

'Goodness, you perform open heart surgery and they moan you're not doing enough. If something untoward happened, they'd be the first to blame us for letting him go home. You'd think they'd just be grateful Robert's well. So much for Christmas spirit.'

'Speaking of Christmas spirit, where's yours?' Ann asked. 'I hear you're snapping at everyone.'

Lucinda pursed her lips. 'I am not,' she stated firmly, then relented. 'Well, maybe I am. I don't know, the nice me didn't seem to get very far.'

'Oh, yes, it did. It got you pregnant with twins,' Ann joked.

'Exactly. Oh, I don't know, Ann, maybe once Seb's gone it will be a bit easier. It's agony, seeing him every day and not being able to tell him.' She sat there glumly. 'On second thoughts, who am I kidding? It's going to be hell when he leaves. As much as I avoid him, it's nice knowing he's around. I just can't imagine not seeing him.'

Ann gave her a knowing look. 'Well, you'd better do something about it. Have you told your parents yet?'

Lucinda shook her head. 'There never seems a good

time. I'll probably get Christmas out of the way first. I don't want to ruin it for them.'

'They're not children, Lucinda. It's not as if you're telling them Father Christmas isn't real. I think now would be an excellent time. From what you've told me, their lives will be one big party over Christmas. It might be just the time to slip in the news, when they're not going to be sitting dwelling over things.'

Lucinda laughed at the idea. 'I don't think so. Can you just imagine? ''Well, happy Christmas for tomorrow. You enjoy your party tonight, and by the way your prodigy is about to become a single parent and you're going to be grandparents to twins. Say hi to the Merringtons for me.''' Lucinda shook her head. 'I'll probably fly up there in the new year once the prof is back. I'll have a couple of annual leave days by then.'

Ann gave her a dry smile. 'Oh, well, it's up to you, but you're going to have to let people know soon. You're starting to show.'

'Surely not,' Lucinda said, shocked. 'I thought that didn't happen for ages yet!' Standing up, she pulled her dress against her stomach. 'I just look a bit bloated.'

Ann laughed. 'I meant a bit higher up. You look as if you've had breast implants.'

'Awful, aren't they? I think I'm going to have to take myself off to Bianca's bra shop for a fitting,' Lucinda joked, but suddenly Ann shivered, and her face paled. 'Are you all right, Ann?'' Lucinda asked, concerned.

Ann gave her a worried look. 'I think so. I just went all cold, as if someone walked over my grave.'

'You're not getting one of your hunches, are you?' Lucinda asked, genuinely concerned.

Ann shook her head. 'I hope not. Still, I'll check the

patients carefully. It'd be awful to have one go off over Christmas.'

'I'll let you get on, then.' Lucinda stood up. 'Are you on in the morning?'

'Yes, just till one.'

'I'll say happy Christmas tomorrow, then.'

The evening stretched out before her. Home didn't sound tempting, but if she went to the doctors' mess she'd probably end up seeing Seb. Suddenly, for the first time in weeks she actually felt hungry. An evening at Suriyan's sounded good and then she could head home to watch 'Carols by Candlelight'. She made her way to the office to collect her bag, but typically now she had decided what to do with herself a spanner was thrown into the works as her emergency pager went off and the overhead system crackled.

'Cardithoracics to Emergency Department. ETA five minutes.'

Lucinda made her way across the hospital. ETA meant the expected arrival time so the paramedics must be bringing someone in. These were the patients she dreaded most. Usually desperately ill and requiring urgent intervention, in the emergency department more than anywhere you had to think on your feet.

She headed straight for the resuscitation room where a collection of staff was waiting around the empty resuscitation bed. Jack Wells greeted her.

'MVA with a penetrating chest injury. Paramedics said it was pretty bad.'

Lucinda nodded. 'Set up for a chest drain and have an emergency thoracotomy tray ready,' she said to the charge nurse.

'Done.'

Lucinda gave a small nod. Here the staff were incredibly

efficient. They made idle chit-chat, used to the drama, but Lucinda didn't join in. Instead, she focussed on the job ahead, aware that to the rest of the staff she probably looked aloof. The charge nurse handed her a lead gown to wear during the resuscitation so that X-rays could be taken without all the staff having to leave the patient.

'G'day, guys. What's the story?'

Seb, breathless from the run, took his place at the head of the bed, slipping on a lead gown while the charge nurse gave him the available details.

Seb listened intently as he set up his equipment. 'Fifteen years old, you said?' He started to pull up some drugs, carefully strapping the ampoules to the syringes so he would have all he needed easily to hand. 'Just the one coming in?'

The charge nurse nodded. 'Just the one. He's the passenger. The driver died at the scene.'

Lucinda felt the usual butterflies around Seb, but as soon as the paramedics wheeled in the teenager all of that was put to one side as she concentrated solely on the patient.

The accident and emergency consultant took the lead. 'On my count.'

The patient was deftly lifted onto the resuscitation bed and a swift assessment was made. Seb checked the airway and sucked out the secretions then introduced an endotracheal tube. Lucinda examined the chest while listening to the paramedics.

'It wasn't a penetrating wound, as we first thought, just a branch, very superficial. But he's got decreased breath sounds on the left.' Lucinda nodded.

'He's tight,' Seb said.

'X-ray.' The radiographer called his warning and everyone not in lead gowns made their way briefly out of the examination room. Lucinda hesitated, torn for a moment.

She knew the lead gown protected her but she didn't want to expose the babies unnecessarily. Once her pregnancy was out in the open there would be no question of her staying, but to leave now could raise a few eyebrows. But now was such a vital stage in the pregnancy and the babies had to come first.

She made her way outside and grabbed the arm of one of the paramedics that had brought the boy in.

'Was it a parent with him that died?'

The paramedic shook his head. 'No, another kid. Wayne Blackwell. He had his licence on him. Only got his P Plates last week. Such a bloody waste.'

The resuscitation doors slid open.

'All clear.'

Lucinda stepped inside and Jack looked up from the patient.

'Where did you disappear to?'

She could feel Seb's eyes on her.

'I just wanted to check something with the paramedics.' It was a bit of a feeble excuse but Jack just nodded.

'He's tight,' Seb stated again.

'I'll put a chest tube in. Here are the films now.'

The films confirmed her suspicions—a massive haemopneumothorax.

It took Lucinda only seconds to insert the chest tube. There was no time for local anaesthetic and no need as the patient was deeply unconscious. Fresh blood poured down the tube.

They all worked together, each with his or her own skills and specialities but united in their efforts to save this young life. 'I'd like him up in Theatre as soon as possible,' Lucinda said, examining the films more closely.

'Sure,' the accident and emergency consultant said. 'The surgeons are happy with his abdomen, but his pelvis is shattered. Neuro want a quick CAT scan before he goes up. Is that all right?'

Lucinda nodded. 'I'll go ahead and scrub.'

She raced ahead up to the theatres where the staff were already setting up.

Once her hands were scrubbed the theatre sister helped her into a gown. 'He's on his way up, no name as yet. Apparently he's got a large subdural haematoma—he just blew a pupil.'

'What a mess.' But there was no time to dwell on it. Seconds later the young boy was wheeled in and together they continued their efforts to save him. The neurosurgeons performed an urgent craniotomy to evacuate the blood clot that was pressing on his brain. Lucinda performed a thoracotomy and repaired a large laceration on his pulmonary vein. Seb monitored his vital signs closely, relaying his messages clearly to the theatre nurses and surgeons, yet he still managed to find the time to talk soothingly to his patient.

Finally the mammoth operation was over and wearily Lucinda made her way to the recovery area, where Seb was still with the patient before his transfer to PICU.

'Have we got a name yet?' she asked the nurse.

'Humpty Dumpty for now, but the police are apparently coming up. They've got some details.'

'All right. When they get hold of the parents, page me. I'm going to have a quick shower.'

Aiming the hot water onto her neck, Lucinda felt the tension in her shoulders start to melt.

Stupid kid, she thought, but not unkindly. She tried to put aside the image of the police knocking on his parents' door on Christmas Eve of all nights. Replacing the soap, she closed her eyes as she thought of the other boy, the one that hadn't even made it to casualty. Wrapping a towel around her, she stepped out of the shower, to find Seb standing there. The showers were unisex but she couldn't help feeling embarrassed to see him, yet one look at his angst-ridden face and she knew the sight of her half-naked was the furthermost thing from his mind.

'What's wrong?' she asked, feeling the hairs stand up on the back of her neck. 'It's not Billy?' she begged.

Seb shook his head slowly. 'No, it's not Billy, thank God. Lucinda, that boy we just operated on—his name is Jake. Jake Benton. He's Ann's son.'

Lucinda's hands flew to her face and she covered her eyes. This was the worst nightmare for all hospital personnel—that it might be a member of your family wheeled in. For Lucinda, having her family in Queensland had allayed that fear, but she had felt a stab of it that day when Billy had been readmitted and he wasn't even her son. How on earth would Ann be feeling?

'No, oh, no. Poor Ann. Does she know?' The towel she had wrapped around her started to slip and Seb gently pulled it tight, covering her. She was vaguely aware of feeling grateful to him for protecting her dignity. He steered her to the little wooden bench where she shakingly sat down.

'Not yet. She's still on the ward. We only just found out. I'm going to go across now. I thought I'd better warn you.'

Lucinda gulped. 'She had a sort of premonition something was wrong. I just assumed it was one of the patients. I never dreamt...'

'How could you have?' he said gently.

Lucinda took a deep breath. 'I'll come with you. You don't want to do that on your own.'

Seb looked into her eyes. 'Are you sure? It's not going to be very pleasant.'

Lucinda stared back. She longed to rest her head on his

chest, longed for him to put his arms around her, but instead she nodded simply. 'Ann's my friend. I should be there for her. She'd do the same for me.'

Seb stood up and, opening the linen cupboard, pulled out a pair of theatre greens and politely turned his back. 'Get dressed quickly, then. You know how gossip spreads. I don't want her finding out by accident.'

They made their way across the hospital to CGU, Lucinda with her hair dripping down her back. There was no small talk, no planned speeches. They arrived on the ward and with relief saw that Ann was alone in her office.

She smiled when she saw them together, a questioning look crossing her face. Lucinda guessed she must be assuming they were finally together. But when she saw their worried faces, her smile faded.

'What's wrong?' The air hung heavy and Seb cleared his throat.

'There's no easy way to say this, Ann, but I've got some bad news for you.'

Ann stood there, her face paling as she prepared herself for the news.

Seb continued gently. 'Jake has been involved in a motor vehicle accident.'

'Is he…?'

'He's not dead, Ann, but he's been very badly hurt.'

'How badly?' Gently Seb sat her down and, dragging another chair over, sat directly opposite her, taking both her hands in his.

'He was brought in a couple of hours ago. We only just found out it was your son.'

'Seb, tell me what his injuries are.'

He nodded and in the gentlest way possible he went through Jake's horrific injuries. Afterwards he sat there silently, letting the news sink in—not moving, just tenderly holding Ann's hands.

Finally Ann spoke. 'I have to see him.'

'We'll take you there now. The police have gone over to tell Tod.'

She stood up and smoothed her dress, but as she started to walk her legs gave way and Lucinda dashed to help her. 'It's all right, Ann. You lean on us we'll take you to Jake now.'

'The ward,' Ann said vaguely.

'The ward will be fine.' They all looked up as Heather Gibbs, the nurse co-ordinator, arrived, her face a picture of concern. 'You go and see your son.'

They walked with Ann to the theatre recovery area. Normally relatives weren't allowed in there when patients were so critical, but in this case no one was going to make a fuss.

Seb took control and managed to say all the right things, and Lucinda realised he could empathise to some extent with what Ann was feeling for he, too, had stood there, looking at his own son. Lucinda busied herself, checking the monitors and drug sheets and IV orders.

'We're going to transfer him over to PICU now,' the theatre sister said, and Ann nodded.

'I'll go and see if Tod's here.' She bent and gave Jake a gentle kiss on his cheek.

'Hang in there, Jake,' she said through her tears, and looked over to where Seb and Lucinda stood. 'I'm glad you two were on tonight. How long are you on, Seb?'

'All night.'

Ann gave a worried look. 'But you're not supposed to be. I've seen the roster. What about Billy?'

'Ann, Billy's with Gemma, and I'm only doing what you did for me. I couldn't be anywhere else.' He gave her a brief hug. 'Now, you go with Lucinda and find Tod. I'll stay with Jake. I promise I won't leave his side. We're going to get you through this, Ann. Stop worrying about everybody else.'

As a doctor, once Theatre was over there wasn't much more Lucinda could do for the time being, but as a friend there was plenty. Seb, as good as his word, parked himself on a stool by Jake's bedside and stayed there all night while Lucinda helped Ann. Dialling phone numbers when her hand was shaking too much, fetching her coffee, and Panadol when she developed the most awful migraine. Taking her husband Tod out onto the roof for a cigarette when it all became too much. And somehow together they made it through the endless night.

'Thought you could use this.' Lucinda stirred from a light doze.

Seb handed her a steaming cup and Lucinda took a grateful sip.

'Yum. Where did you get a cappuccino on Christmas morning? Is the canteen having a party?'

'I bunged one of the orderlies a few dollars and he headed over to Southbank. A lot of the restaurants are doing Christmas lunch so they're open.'

'You should have bunged him a bit more and got some muffins,' Lucinda said in a grumbling voice, but Seb knew she was only joking.

'Lucindah, have you any idea the damage a single muffin can do to your thighs?'

It was a perfect impersonation of her mother and Lucinda managed a smile. 'How's Jake? Any change?'

Seb shrugged. 'No change, but I guess no news is good news at the moment. We're just going to have to play the waiting game. Are you going to go home and have a rest? You look exhausted, Lucinda.' He sounded concerned.

'I'll stay. I can always go to one of the on-call rooms if I'm getting in the way.'

'That's the last thing you're doing. You've been a great help to Ann. You two are really close, aren't you?'

'She's hard not to like.'

He picked up the cardboard tray with the coffees. 'I guess it's not really appropriate to say merry Christmas, given the circumstances, but you know what I mean.'

'I know,' she said softly. 'But it is a time for miracles.'

'Let's hope so,' Seb said solemnly, and made his way back onto PICU.

She sat there awhile, drinking her coffee, and though her thoughts were with Ann her mind drifted to Seb. His had been the first face she had woken up to on Christmas morning and the only face she ever wanted to wake up to, but their time had been and gone. It might be a time for miracles, she thought sadly, but it would be selfish to wish for two, and of them both, Jake was probably the safer bet.

CHAPTER TEN

DESPITE the sweltering weather, it was the bleakest of Christmases. Lucinda duly rang home and tried but failed miserably to inject any enthusiasm into her voice. Not that Abigail appeared to notice.

'Guess what your father got me for Christmas?'

'I have no idea.'

'No, go on, try and guess.'

'Just tell me, Mum,' Lucinda said wearily, her mind on far more important things.

'Spoilsport. Well, you'd never have guessed anyway. We're going skiing in Europe—doesn't that sound so-o glamorous? It was a huge surprise. Your father got our secretary involved and together they've rigged it so we've got a full three weeks off. I can't wait.'

'You're going skiing? Mum, you've never even seen snow.'

'Goodness, no, Lucinda. I may be going skiing but I certainly won't be doing any, perish the thought. Could you imagine the havoc a fall could wreak at my age? Not that I look it, of course. I went for a check-up last month and my darling GP said I had the body of a thirty-year-old.'

'Which one?' Lucinda tried to joke, but her mother wasn't listening.

'Anyway, apparently the après-ski is simply *très bien*, so France, here I come.'

Lucinda managed a laugh. 'No doubt your winter wardrobe will cost more than the plane tickets.'

'Of course, darling, you have to look the part. Lucinda,

you are all right, aren't you?' her mother asked suddenly. 'You're not feeling homesick or anything?'

Lucinda paused, momentarily stunned that her mother had even noticed. 'I'm fine, Mum. We had some bad news at the hospital overnight.'

Abigail seemed to accept her explanation. 'Oh, dear. I was actually just thinking this morning, do you realise this is the first Christmas that we haven't seen each other? Not that we're a turkey-and-singing-round-the-tree-type family, but we've always managed at least a glass of champers together. I suppose you were too busy to notice. It was just a thought, that's all.'

Lucinda found herself smiling into the telephone. 'I was actually thinking just the same thing.'

After hanging up, she sat for a few moments, just staring at the telephone. It took a few seconds to register that Seb had come into the room.

'Are you all right?'

Lucinda looked up. 'I was just talking to my mum. Funny, she actually sounded as if she was missing me. I must be going soft or something. I'm actually missing them.'

Seb smiled. 'That's what families do to you. Can't live with them, can't live without them. I just spoke to Billy.'

'How is he? Did you manage to get a word in?'

Seb gave a small shrug 'He told me everything Santa had bought him and all that, but he was a bit teary.'

'Is it your first Christmas apart?'

Seb gave a small nod. 'I'm normally on call more often than not, but it's very different to being thousands of kilometres away. Not that the last few years have been particularly joyous occasions, but we at least managed to put on a united front for Billy's sake.'

She ventured a little further, she simply had to know more. 'How are things going now with Billy and Gemma?'

'Good, touch wood.' He reached over to the small coffee-table. 'Now she doesn't have the daily grind, as she called it, she actually seems to be enjoying motherhood—in small portions, mind. She'll soon have had enough but at least this way Billy feels like he's got a mum who cares, even if it is only in short bursts.'

Lucinda stood up. She had wanted to know but it simply hurt too much. 'I'm going to have a shower.'

'Lucinda?'

She turned.

'I couldn't help but notice yesterday when I came and got you from the theatre showers.' Lucinda held her breath. Surely he hadn't noticed anything. But she had to think on her feet when Seb continued, 'You were wearing the robot Billy bought you on your necklace.' Seb's eyes searched her face for a reaction and Lucinda opened her eyes wide, feigning surprise.

'Was I really?' She pulled her chain out from inside her theatre top. 'So I am. I must have forgotten to take it off after he gave it to me.'

'It'll turn your chest green.'

As she walked to the showers she let out a sigh. That had been a bit too close. What would Seb have said if he'd known the truth? That she'd actually gone to a jewellers and had had the tiny little robot heavily gold plated the same day Billy had given it to her, after it had indeed left a large dirty green streak in her cleavage. Lucinda had probably spent a hundred times its original price but it had been worth every last cent. Somehow, wearing it, she felt closer to them both. Silly maybe, but who ever said love was sensible?

After her shower she made her way back to PICU, just

in time to see Ann coming out. 'I was just coming to see you. How's things?'

Ann looked grey. Her uniform had been replaced by some theatre greens and her eyes were swollen and puffy.

'No change,' she said wearily. 'Tod wants me to go and lie down but I don't want to leave Jake.'

'I know you don't,' Lucinda said sympathetically. 'But Tod's right. You haven't slept in over twenty-four hours, Ann. You have to get some rest.'

'I couldn't sleep. Every time I close my eyes I see his face…' Her voice was rising and Lucinda could hear the note of hysteria creeping in.

'I'll get you something to help you sleep.'

'I don't want to be knocked out. What if I don't hear? What if there's any change?'

'Ann.' Lucinda's voice was firm without being unkind. 'I'm not going to give you a general anaesthetic, just 10 mg of temazepam. It's only light, it will just help you to rest. Now, Jake's going to need you to be strong—Tod, too. We can't have you fainting all over the place. What help will that be to Jake?'

Ann seemed to accept this and Lucinda led her to one of the on-call rooms where Ann, calmer now, lay on the bed.

'Just wait here. I'll be back in five.'

She walked to CGU where Ellen was on the telephone. Hastily she finished her call. 'What can I do for you, Miss Chambers?'

'Can you give me 10 mg of temazepam? Ann needs to sleep. I'll sign for it.'

Ellen got her keys out of her pocket and opened the drug cupboard.

'There you go. Tell her that we're all thinking of her. If there's anything we can do, you will let us know?'

Lucinda nodded as she signed the drug book. 'At this stage all we can do is wait and hope, but thanks for this. If she can get a couple of hours rest it will be a big help.'

Lucinda filled a polystyrene cup from the sink and Ann swallowed the pill meekly.

'Now, once you're resting I'll go and tell the PICU staff and Tod what room you're in. Of course they'll come and get you if anything changes, but Jake's stable at the moment, Ann. Tomorrow or the day after, when they extubate him, we'll know a lot more. You need to keep your strength up for then. Now, close your eyes.'

But she didn't. She lay there and with brimming eyes stared directly at Lucinda. 'One minute they're babies and the next... I don't know where the time goes. Before you know it they're teenagers and they think they're invincible. I know he did the wrong thing but he's still my baby. He didn't deserve this. What if it had been Jake that died? I don't think I could have gone on.'

'Shh,' Lucinda soothed. 'It wasn't Jake. You just have to be grateful for that.'

The pill was starting to take effect and Ann's eyes grew heavy. 'Don't let Seb go without knowing, Lucinda. Your babies deserve a father. I couldn't do this without Tod. You'd be so good together, I just know.'

Lucinda sat there with tears rolling down her cheeks but Ann was too out of it to notice. 'Don't worry about that now, Ann,' she said in a shaking voice. 'You sleep now.'

Finally Ann drifted off and Lucinda sat there until she was sure Ann wasn't about to wake up. Tiptoeing out of the room, she gently closed the door and made her way over to PICU. Seb was checking Jake's pupil reaction. Tod was holding his son's hand. Carols were belting merrily from the radio, but not loud enough to drown the hiss of the ventilators and the bleeping of the monitors. 'Joy To The World'.

What joy? she thought angrily, and then checked herself. The last thing she wanted to become was bitter. Yet it was the most ironic of scenes—sad because Jake and the other children here were so desperately ill on Christmas day of all days. Sad because Seb was without his son today, and unaware of the twins she was carrying.

But in some ways if it wasn't happy exactly, there was an air of hope. A feeling of quiet efficiency, guarded optimism for these young lives surrounded by dedicated staff and family that cared. There was joy, too, for her, and Lucinda acknowledged that next Christmas, God willing, she would be spending it with her babies. Seb looked up as she stood there and Lucinda managed a small smile.

'Ann's asleep. She's in on-call 2.'

Seb nodded. 'Why don't you go home, too, Lucinda? Grab some shut-eye. You look completely worn out.'

'I'd rather be here,' she said.

'Take your own advice, Lucinda. Who knows what's going to come through the doors of A and E? You need to rest while you can.'

Lucinda nodded. He was right, of course. And so she collected her bag and without bothering even to change she walked back to her flat, still dressed in her theatre gear. As she wearily let herself in she headed straight for her bed. Too tired to even pull back the covers, she lay on the top and, closing her eyes, for once she went straight to sleep.

The ringing of the telephone broke into her dreamless sleep. Fuddled, she reached for the receiver.

'Lucinda, darling.'

'Mum?' She sat up. 'What time is it?'

'About eight. Your father's had too much brandy and is

snoring away. Such a revolting sight. I thought I'd ring you.'

'Is everything all right?' Lucinda asked cautiously. Never in living memory had she been on the phone to her mother twice in the same week, let alone twice on the same day!

'That's what I was about to ask you. I know you said things had been a bit grim at the hospital, but I can't help thinking there's something else wrong. You can talk to me, you know. I am your mother.'

Abigail's concern caught Lucinda completely off guard and she sat silently on the bed, holding the telephone.

'Lucinda, are you still there? Say something,' her mother demanded.

'I'm pregnant, Mum.'

It was Abigail's turn to be silent. Lucinda heard her intake of breath and found she was holding her breath as well.

'You're what?' Abigail gasped a moment later, and Lucinda could hear the absolute horror in her mother's voice. 'You are joking, I hope.'

Lucinda didn't reply but it didn't matter. Her mother had plenty to say. 'So who's the father—that anaesthetist you brought to lunch?'

'Yes, Mum, but we're not together any more. He's moving to the country with his son.'

'Oh, he is, is he? Well, we'll soon see about that. You're not going to have it, are you?'

'Of course I am,' Lucinda cried.

'My goodness. This sort of thing happens to teenage girls, not women in their thirties. You're both doctors, for heaven's sake. Didn't you learn about birth control in medical school? How,' she asked, 'do you expect to look after it? It's simply not feasible. You've got your career to think of.'

They were the same questions Lucinda had been battling with. She fought back her tears. Oh, well, she might as well tell her all of it.

'I'm having twins, Mum.'

'My God, Lucinda. Well, this just gets better and better. Twins! What is Seb—some sort of hippy guru that goes around impregnating women? Can't he take the twins to the country with him and his precious son, and they can all live in their commune together?'

'Mum, you're being silly,' Lucinda said, but Abigail hadn't finished yet.

'No, you're being silly, Lucinda. All those years at the best private schools, *the* top medical school and a career going somewhere, and you're about to throw it all away— for what? If you think I'm going to babysit, think again. I've done my child-rearing. What am I going to tell everyone? It's just so, well, embarrassing.'

Lucinda had listened to enough. Anger rose within her. Hell, she hadn't expected an easy ride when she told her mother but a little bit of encouragement wouldn't have gone amiss.

'You can tell your friends what ever you like. I really couldn't care less what they think. And don't worry. I wasn't counting on you to be around to help. It's not as if you've much experience with babies.'

'What's that supposed to mean?' Abigail interrupted furiously.

'Well, how many of my nappies did you change, Mum? You certainly didn't put your career on hold for me. Why would you do it for your grandchildren?'

'How dare you speak to your mother like that?'

'Mum, I have to go.' Lucinda said.

'I haven't finished yet.'

'Well, I have.' She put down the phone and then, after

checking her pager was working, took the telephone off the hook. With a sigh she lay back on the bed. Her hands instinctively reached down and gently she massaged her stomach.

She'd told her mother and, as expected, Abigail had signed herself off the help roster. Ann, however much she might have wanted to help, wasn't going to be able to now. And Seb, well, he had to get his life sorted with Billy.

'Don't worry,' she said in a trembling voice to the babies inside her. 'We'll manage.' Her voice wavered. 'We'll do fine by ourselves.'

Jake was gradually weaned off the ventilator. It took longer than had been hoped and he was still disorientated and confused from his head injury, but the neurosurgeons were cautiously optimistic that this would resolve over the coming days and there would be no residual brain damage. His chest drain was removed and finally he was transferred to the orthopaedic ward where his shattered pelvis would keep him in bed for the next few weeks.

For Ann and Tod the days were endless the nights even longer. They had the unenviable task of going to the other boy's funeral, and when Lucinda saw Ann when she returned from the service she was shocked by how much Ann seemed to have aged.

'They'll turn you grey,' Lucinda remembered her joking to Seb. It seemed that Ann, yet again, had been proved right.

For Lucinda, too, the days were torture. Seb's departure grew ever more imminent and she felt a growing panic. Was she doing the wrong thing in not telling him? Billy's robot still hung around her neck. Not only was she depriving Seb of his children but Billy of his half-brothers or -sisters. What right did she have to do that? The agony of indecision weighed heavily on her. So many times she was tempted to tell him, but it never seemed the right time. Her throat would go dry and Seb would give her a quizzical look until she made some excuse as to why she had said she needed to see him.

New Year's Eve found her sitting alone in her flat with the balcony doors open. She could hear the trams clattering by, carrying revellers to their various parties, hear the joyous calls of partygoers. It only served to make her feel even more alone. With a sigh she pulled the balcony door closed. The intercom buzzing caught her unawares. With a surge of hope she thought it might be Seb and then checked herself. It was probably just the neighbours to warn her of a noisy party. Never did it enter her head that it might be Abigail.

'Mum, what on earth are you doing here?'

Abigail brushed past her. 'Before the big speeches I simply must lie down.' She made her way dramatically over to the sofa. 'Get me some pillows—quickly, Lucinda,' she ordered.

Lucinda rushed to her bed and grabbed the pillows. Whatever was wrong? Anxiously she tucked the pillows behind her mother's head.

'Not there, Lucinda. Put them under my legs.'

'But why?' Lucinda demanded. 'Mum, what on earth's wrong?'

'My ankles have swollen. Look at the size of them. I have to elevate them. If a few hours on a plane from Queensland can do this, what am I going to be like when we go to France?' Lucinda hid a smile as her mother continued. 'Mind you, we'll be flying first class so I can keep my legs up all the way. I had to slum it in economy to get here. All the decent seats were taken—can you imagine?'

'I've only ever flown economy,' Lucinda said truthfully, 'and I've never had a problem.'

Abigail screwed up her nose.

'But, Mum, what are you doing here, on New Year's Eve of all nights? I thought you were going on a cruise on the river.'

Abigail waved her hand. 'Never mind about some silly cruise. I've come to apologise to my baby.'

Lucinda's jaw dropped.

'Don't look so shocked—I can admit when I'm wrong.'

'I'm sorry too, Mum,' Lucinda said graciously. 'It must have been an awful shock.'

'You can say that again. Your poor father's still on the brandy.'

'Is he very upset?' Lucinda asked nervously.

'No. Isn't that the strangest thing? He's completely stunned, but aren't we all? Your father, once he got over the initial surprise, is actually delighted, keeps wanting to celebrate. I'm not quite there yet but I'm coming along. It will just take some getting used to. I actually read an article on the plane about supermodels who deliberately have a baby without a man, well, not completely—you know, a one-night stand or IVF. It's apparently quite trendy.'

Lucinda tried not to laugh. 'Mum, I'm not a supermodel.'

'Well, you could have been if you'd wanted to. I got you a present. Pass me my bag.'

Lucinda did as she was told and Abigail handed her a huge jar of cream.

'You have to massage it in three times a day—religiously, mind. It will help to prevent stretch marks.'

'Mum, you know as well as I do that nothing can prevent stretch marks.'

'Well, it's worth a try and, let's face it, you need all the help you can get. Have you any idea the havoc twins will wreak on your body? But don't worry, darling. I couldn't operate on my own baby but I'm sure Malcolm will give you a free abdominoplasty. He's a great surgeon. He's done a few things for me but that's my little secret.'

All Lucinda could do was laugh. 'Mum, you're completely crazy, do you know that?'

'I know. You've obviously had an ultrasound?'

Lucinda unpinned the photo from the fridge and handed it to Abigail.

'Golly,' she said as she stared at the photo. 'There really are two in there. But that's just like us Chambers, isn't it? We don't do anything by halves. Look at you, Lucinda, good-looking, clever and incredibly fertile.' She gave Lucinda a wink and patted the sofa beside her. 'Come and sit down and tell me all about it.'

And so she did, telling her all. Abigail surprised even herself by actually listening for once, and when the clock struck midnight they stood on the balcony together, watching the fireworks light up the Melbourne sky line.

'Happy New Year, Mum.'

Happy New Year, Lucinda. It's going to be a big year for you, for all of us really. I can't believe I'm going to be a grandmother.'

Lucinda nodded, watching as a rocket soared upwards. 'I'm scared, Mum.'

'Lucinda Chambers!' her mother barked. 'Stand up straight and take a deep breath. You can handle anything.' It was the same line she had used over and over when it had been time to go back to boarding school or Lucinda's exams had been about to begin, but this time Abigail reached out and took hold of her daughter's hand, her voice softening as she continued, 'I'm here now. We'll get there.'

Those few days with her mother were precious. Instead of reminding Lucinda of the calorific value of each mouth-

ful she ate, Abigail went and bought a blender and mag-
icked up wicked mango and banana smoothies, adding huge
dollops of ice cream to welcome Lucinda's returning ap-
petite. But all too soon it was time for her to leave. Lucinda
sat on the bed, watching as her mother packed with military
precision, separating each carefully folded article with layer
upon layer of tissue paper. Even her undies were individ-
ually wrapped.

'I really feel awful, leaving you,' Abigail said as she
collected up her numerous creams from the dressing-table.
'Are you sure you don't want me to ring your father and
cancel the skiing? We can go any time.'

Lucinda shook her head. 'Please, don't, Mum.'

'But it's Seb's leaving party tonight. I should be here for
you.'

'I'll be fine. You go and have a great time.'

'I might head off to Paris while I'm there—see what I
can get for the twins. The French are so chic. Their babies
must be, too.' She turned then, her face suddenly serious.

'Seb has to know, Lucinda. I agree it might be better to
let him get settled into his new home but you'll have to
tell him soon.'

'I know, Mum. Just let me get tonight over with and then
I'll work something out.'

'Do you really have to go tonight? It might be a bit much
for you.'

'I'll be fine and, anyway, I've got no choice. I'm expected to be there. I'll just go for a couple of drinks to be
seen.'

Abigail closed her case and checked the straps. 'You're
sure you don't want me to stay.'

'Positive.'

Despite her declarations, Lucinda was anything but fine.
Seb had served the hospital well over the years and in re-

turn he was being given a big send-off. The party was being held in the doctors' mess and everyone had chipped in. All the guests had a list of what bottle to bring so cocktails could be mixed.

Lucinda made her way up the steps. Despite the warm night, she shivered in her flimsy dress, a grey chiffon with shoestring straps that flowed gently and covered the tell-tale bulge that was definitely, despite what the books said, starting to show already. It was the only dress in her ward-robe that fitted well, and she just hoped the thin straps held up against the weight of her ever-increasing bosom.

Handing over her bottle, she looked anxiously around the room.

'Lucinda.' Pete marched over. 'Have you heard?'

'What?'

Pete was grinning like a Cheshire cat. 'Mr Felix isn't coming back and the prof has had a quiet word to me. He's going to speak to you, too.'

Lucinda stared back at him. 'You mean…'

'That's right,' Pete said triumphantly, 'I've finally made it. And wait until you hear what they've got in store for you. I hope your passport's up to date.'

Lucinda managed to smile but inside her heart sunk. It meant she was going to have to tell the professor sooner rather that later. It was just another thing to worry about on top of everything else.

'It's supposed to be hush-hush,' Pete carried on, 'but everyone knows. I've already had four champagnes thrust at me.'

Lucinda smiled, genuinely this time. 'You deserve it, Pete. Now, what are you going to do about that woman of yours?'

Pete smiled. 'Well, now, I might just have to make an honest woman of her.'

Lucinda leant over and gave him a kiss on the cheek. 'I want an invitation to the wedding, remember. I love wearing a hat.'

'The speeches are about to start. I must go and find Ellen. Come over and sit with us.'

'I'll just stand here and listen, thanks, Pete. I'll be over in a bit.'

'You're sure? Can I get you a drink, then?'

Lucinda gave him a smile. 'I'm fine, Pete. Go and find Ellen.' He made his way across the room as the lights dimmed and everyone hushed. She wanted to be alone for this and she listened with tears sparkling in her eyes as colleague after colleague spoke about Seb. Everyone here had known him for longer than her, and she couldn't help but feel a stab of jealousy as they recounted stories about him, tales from his past where she didn't belong. She listened quietly as they wished him well for the future where she didn't fit in either. All the speeches came down to the same thing—Seb was a rare blend indeed, compassionate and caring but funny, too, a wonderful man, a brilliant doctor, and everyone would miss him. She could second that.

And then it was Seb's turn to speak. Taking the microphone, he looked his usual confident self, but she could hear the emotion in his voice as he thanked everyone for coming.

'You've been a great team to work with over the years. But it's been so much more than just work with you guys. You've all been there for me through all the ups and downs with Billy, and I know there's been more than enough drama there. Hopefully now things can settle down for both of us but, rest assured, we'll come back and visit often. We're going to miss you all, too.'

For a second Lucinda thought his eyes met hers but his gaze travelled past her. She stood there quite still, memorising every detail of his beautiful face, the face that might be apparent in the features of his children. How could she stand here and watch him leave? How could she just stand there and let him walk out of her life when there was so much that needed to be said?

And then it hit her. It was because she loved him and Billy, too, that she was letting them go, letting them have this time to get their lives together before she complicated things yet again for them. Letting them have a breathing space to settle in before she turned their worlds upside down. Seb didn't love her enough, didn't think she was up to being a stepmother to Billy. When she saw him again she would have things worked out, be able to give him the news without breaking down, without telling him how much she loved him, leaving him free to get on with his own life.

She held onto that thought and when Seb replaced the microphone in its stand and left the stage it was the only thing that stopped her rushing over to him.

'We should be here waving the two of you off together. You're not just going to let him go, are you?'

Lucinda swung around and there was Ann. 'I have to, Ann, but I am going to tell him.'

'When?'

'In a couple of months or so. By then I'll be more sure of how I'm going to cope. It will be easier telling him if I at least know what my plans are.' She swallowed hard a couple of times and then managed a smile. 'I didn't expect to see you here.'

'I couldn't let Seb go without a proper goodbye, and nor should you.'

'It's just not that simple,' Lucinda argued, but Ann wasn't giving in.

'It's as simple as you want it to be. You're having his

babies, Lucinda. I know what he said, but I'm sure he didn't mean it, not Seb. He's special and—'

But Lucinda cut her off. 'Just leave it, Ann, please.' Ann nodded but Lucinda could tell there was plenty more she wanted to say. 'How's Jake?' Lucinda asked, glad to be able to change the subject.

'Sore and sorry. He's got a long road ahead of him but he'll be all right. I'm just waiting for him to get a bit more strength back and then I can kill him,' she said dryly.

'And how are you coping with it all?'

Ann gave a small shrug. 'Every time it gets too hard, I just think of Wayne's parents and think what they're going through. I know then that I'm the lucky one. It's made me do a bit of thinking, though. I've taken long-service leave, I had twelve weeks owing, but after that I think I'll hand my notice in.'

Lucinda had half expected to hear it. Ann had already hinted she'd had enough at the Christmas party and now, given all that had happened, she wasn't surprised.

'The ward will really miss you, Ann. Me, too.'

'I'll miss them as well, but sometimes family just has to come first, as you're no doubt about to find out. I'm not against working mums. I'm one myself. And although we've needed my wage, I've also loved my career, but sometimes you have to stop and smell the roses. Some things just have to give when you have children. Anyway, with the way Jake is, I'll be around the hospital for a while yet so you're not going to get a chance to miss me. And that means I can keep an eye on you, make sure you do tell him.'

'You don't give up, do you?' Lucinda smiled.

'Only when it's a lost cause, and I certainly don't think that about you and Seb. Speaking of which, I'd better go and find him—I want to get back up to Jake.'

Ann made her way over and Lucinda watched as Seb, who was chatting away, stopped and greeted his friend, obviously touched and delighted she'd made the effort to come. He put his arm casually around Ann's shoulders and drew her into the group. The hospital was losing two of its finest.

Lucinda lingered a moment, not wanting to leave, but how could she stay? She had made an appearance—that was enough. If she had to speak to him, had to go over and say goodbye, she knew she couldn't do it. Turning on her heel, she slipped from the room, unnoticed, and walked out of the party and out of Seb's life. It was the hardest thing she had ever done.

Lucinda didn't go straight home. Instead, she wandered aimlessly along the Yarra, staring into the murky waters, tears streaming unchecked down her cheeks. No one paid her any attention. The riverbank was bursting with couples and groups. The theatres had come out and theatre-goers were walking past, clutching their programmes, stopping for a drink, prolonging the night, so that they could relive the play they had just seen.

She put her hand up to her necklace and clutched the tiny robot, reliving scenes of her own—that weekend in Queensland where no scripts had been needed, when it had all flowed so beautifully. Who could have predicted then how the final scene would have played out? Slowly she made her way across the bridge.

On Monday she would be back at work, but this time there would be no Ann and, more poignantly, no Seb. She would tell Mr Hays that she couldn't accept the promotion Pete had hinted at. It simply wouldn't be fair to take it, knowing that she was going to be taking maternity leave. Maybe she could work part time for a while, and if that didn't work out she could always go into research. What was that saying? Nine to five and no one died. It sounds pretty good from here, she thought wearily as she pushed the revolving doors to her apartment block.

'Lucinda.' Standing in her lobby was Seb.

She blinked a couple of times. 'What are you doing here?' she finally managed to ask.

'I've just been speaking to Ann. We need to talk.'

She nodded, her heart in her mouth. Seb pushed the lift button and they stepped inside, Seb watching her as she busied herself retrieving her keys from the depths of her bag.

She let them in and, flicking the lights on, found her voice.

'What did Ann say?' she asked nervously as she set about getting glasses from the kitchen cupboard.

'That I was mad to leave you.'

Ann, it would seem, had been busy.

'Anything else?'

'That I should tell you how I feel.'

She finally looked over to where he stood. For once he didn't look his usual confident self, and Lucinda was reminded of that morning in the annexe after Billy's operation.

'You've already told me how you feel, Seb, right over there by the door, remember, the same door you walked out of a couple of months ago.'

Seb shook his head 'That wasn't how I felt. Walking out that night was the worse thing I've ever had to do, you have to believe me.'

'Then why did you?' She stood there, her back straight, and took a deep breath. Abigail would have been proud.

Seb walked over and took the glasses out of her hands. Placing them on the kitchen bench, he took her hand and guided her over to the couch.

'Can we sit down and talk properly?'

She gave a small nod and sat down, staring ahead as Seb sat beside her. She was terrified her eyes might betray her and he would realise how much she loved him.

'I knew you were a great doctor even before I met you,' he started unsteadily. 'Then, after seeing you work, I knew that you weren't just good, you're probably the best surgeon I've ever seen. You can go as far as you like.'

Lucinda shook her head, and started to stand up. 'What on earth has that got to do with anything?'

'Please, Lucinda.' He pulled her back down beside him. 'Let me finish.

'When you made that speech in Queensland I knew you were going to be huge. Then when I met your parents, heard about your dreams, well, I just don't belong in that world.'

'Nor do I, and what dreams are you talking about?' she interrupted, then stopped as Seb continued.

'When you went to the loo your dad took me to one side. He told me that even from when you were little all you ever wanted to be was the world's best heart surgeon.'

'That was all *they* ever wanted me to be. Why would you listen to what my father says without discussing it with me?'

Seb stood up. 'Maybe I will have that drink'. He went over to the bench and poured out two glasses of wine. Putting down the bottle, he looked across at her.

'It got me thinking. At the conference John McClelland had told me about a chief of anaesthetics position coming up in Ballarat. When I went to the hospital that night, I told you that I'd spoken with Vince about Billy's asthma.'

Lucinda nodded.

'Well, he spelt it out for me. He said Billy needed a lot more stability. It just seemed all the signs were pointing against us. Then when Chris got back from the wedding he said that the prof had been blabbing. Lucinda, I've known since that day that Mr Felix was never coming back, that you were going to make at the very least Senior Consultant, and from the way the prof had been talking he was thinking of sending you to the UK. The hospital felt you were worth the investment, don't you see? You'll be a professor one day.'

'But what's that got to do with us?'

He slammed the glass down on the bench, exasperated.

'Don't be so naïve, Lucinda. It has everything to do with us. In a different place and time maybe we could work things out, survive the distance, work around each other's schedules. But there's Billy to think of. I can't put him through that.'

'Ah, yes,' said Lucinda nastily. 'As you said, I'm not exactly stepmum material.'

'I never said that, Lucinda. They were your words, remember?'

Lucinda swallowed. He was right. It had been her that had said that, but what was the difference? He had been about to finish things.

'Like I said, Billy has to come first,' Seb continued. 'He already adored you. How could I let him get to know you, let him get to love you, knowing it was useless, that you'd go off to the UK, get on with your life. I couldn't put him through that.'

'So why are you here, then? It seems you've already decided I'm not up to the job,' Lucinda said defensively.

'Because I don't think I can do this without you,' came his honest reply. 'I don't think I can get through the next fifty years without you. Ann finally had a go at me. She told me that me and Billy were about to lose the best thing that had ever happened to us if I didn't at least give you the option of coming with us. Look, Lucinda, when you said you weren't up to being a stepmum…'

'I was just saving face,' Lucinda admitted. 'I thought you were trying to end things.'

'Hell, no,' Seb rasped. 'I was just trying to be realistic. I knew we needed to have a long talk.' He took a long drink. 'I've had one failed marriage because of my wife's career, and I was terrified of making a mistake, yet with you I was sure things could be different, that we could somehow work something out. My God, I even considered giving up my work to let you carry on with yours. Have you any idea how that felt? The thought of giving up my career and having you supporting Billy and me! It goes against everything I've been brought up to believe, but if it meant keeping you… Doesn't that show how desperate I was to make things work?

'But when you said it wasn't for you, that it wasn't what you wanted, well, it just seemed pointless. The other stuff we could have worked out in time, but if you didn't, as you said, want Billy…well, he's not an optional item. You had to want both of us.' He looked across at her, his eyes searching her face. 'You really didn't mean what you said?' His voice was tentative at first, but she heard the surge of optimism as he spoke.

She shook her head 'Not a word of it. I adore Billy and I love you,' she gasped. 'I always have.'

'I have to take this job, Lucinda. I have to give Billy this chance.'

'I know you do.'

'And I know I'm mad even asking, I know there's a million reasons why you can't come with me, but I have to ask you. Lucinda, if you can't come I'll understand, and we'll work something out.'

She gazed into Seb's troubled eyes. Here he was, this

beautiful, proud man, putting his son's happiness before his own and in his own jumbled way telling her just how much he loved her, wanted her, needed her.

'So you're asking me to move to the country with you and Billy? To juggle the school runs and packed lunches…'

'Together, we'd work it out together.'

A smile started to flicker across her face. The news she'd been so dreading telling him was now a pleasure.

'There is one small problem—two, actually.'

Seb's face had a pained dignity as he waited for her to deliver the reasons why she couldn't come with him.

'Billy's going to have to get used to sharing me, and I hope that house you told me about has lots of bedrooms. We're going to need them when the twins are born.'

'The twins?' Seb asked, his voice bewildered.

'Our twins,' she said softly. 'They're due in July.'

And as he looked at her glowing, radiant face, gradually realisation dawned and a smile crept across his weary, strained features. With an incredulous laugh he pulled her towards him, running a tender hand over her swollen, heavy breasts and down to her gently rounded stomach.

'Hey, you really are,' he said in wonder. 'You really are.'

'No, Seb,' Lucinda whispered as he wrapped his arms tightly around her. '*We* are.'

EPILOGUE

'WHAT's burning?'

'Shh.' Lucinda gave a pained look as Seb walked into the kitchen and, putting down his briefcase, gave her a long kiss.

'Mum's *attempting* to bake Billy a birthday cake,' she said finally. 'It's her third go.'

'Why doesn't she just buy one?'

'Because the local baker's range didn't stretch to robots,' Lucinda said matter-of-factly.

Seb ruffled her hair as she pulled off the scarf she had been using to tie it back.

'Any post?'

Lucinda handed him a couple of snapshots. 'Ricky Stewart. Isn't he gorgeous? Janine's beside herself—doesn't even mind the sleepless nights.'

Seb smiled as he looked at the photos. 'He is a cute baby.' He looked back at Lucinda. 'You've been doing some painting?'

'Just the fretwork on the veranda. I'm saving the big jobs for you. I'll come up with you and get changed.'

'Mum, watch the children,' she called as she made her way up the stairs, with Seb following. 'I'm just going to get out of these work clothes.'

Watching her peel off her paint-splattered dungarees, Seb felt weak in the knees with longing as he admired her full breasts encased in cream lace. Her body, always gorgeous, was softer now and more curvaceous despite Lucinda's heroic but sporadic post-pregnancy dieting attempts.

'Come here,' he said huskily, pulling her towards him.

Lucinda, laughing, wriggled out of his embrace. 'Mum's downstairs.'

'She won't even notice we're gone with the kids about. Have you told her yet?'

Lucinda nodded. The local GP had offered her a position at his practice. Very part time for now—alternate Saturday or Sunday mornings and one evening clinic a week. The hours would increase in later years as he wound down with a view to retirement. Lucinda had jumped at the chance. Though more fulfilled than she had ever been in her life, the chance to use her brain again, practising medicine, *and* still have heaps of time for the children had been accepted like a gift from the gods. But telling her mother had proved difficult. 'She wasn't too keen.'

Seb's face sank. 'I guess it is a big step down from consultant cardiothoracic surgeon to GP.'

'No, silly.' Lucinda threw a pillow at him. 'She had the gall to tell me I should spend more time with the children. "They're only young for five minutes, Lucinda, you should enjoy this precious time."' She mimicked her mother's voice. 'You'd think that she'd won the Mother of the Year award for raising me. I was tempted to point out that she'd barely delivered the placenta before she went back to work.'

'Maybe she realises what she missed out on,' Seb said gently. 'She's really changed, hasn't she?'

'Changed?' Lucinda said incredulously. 'I hardly recognise her.'

'It doesn't upset you?'

'Not a scrap,' she assured him. 'I'm delighted, even if it is over thirty years late.'

Seb's voice was suddenly serious. 'I know what you've given up.'

'Seb, we've been over this. I've never been happier.'

'But still…'

She silenced his doubts with a kiss, and with her soft, fragrant skin pressing against him his uncertainties slowly vanished.

'Look at everything I've gained,' she whispered into his ear. 'You, Billy, Molly and Harry, even Mum.' She kissed him again, deeply this time, until all that was on Seb's mind was how quickly they could get the children and mother-in-law off to bed.

'Someone's coming,' he gasped, pulling away.

Delighted at the effect she had on him, Lucinda laughingly pulled on her bathrobe as Billy entered the bedroom.

'Nanna's taking us to the shop. We need some silver sugar balls for the robot cake's buttons.'

Seb winked at Lucinda. Maybe they wouldn't have to wait till bedtime after all.

'Does she really have to go back to Queensland on Friday?' Billy asked, his big eyes filling with tears.

Seb pulled Billy onto his knee. 'She'll come again soon,' he said comfortingly.

'Honest?' sniffed Billy.

Seb rolled his eyes but his voice was light and Lucinda knew he was only teasing her.

'Oh, you can count on it, sport, you can count on it.'

Modern Romance™
...seduction and
passion guaranteed

Tender Romance™
...love affairs that
last a lifetime

Sensual Romance™
...sassy, sexy and
seductive

Blaze
...sultry days and
steamy nights

Medical Romance™
...medical drama on
the pulse

Historical Romance™
...rich, vivid and
passionate

29 new titles every month.

*With all kinds of Romance for
every kind of mood...*

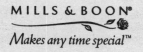

MILLS & BOON®

Makes any time special™

MAT4

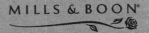

MILLS & BOON®

Christmas
with a Latin Lover

Three brand-new stories

Lynne Graham

Penny Jordan

Lucy Gordon

Published 19th October

*Available at most branches of WH Smith,
Tesco, Martins, Borders, Eason, Sainsbury's,
and most good paperback bookshops.*

4 Books
and a surprise gift!

We would like to take this opportunity to thank you for reading this Mills & Boon® book by offering you the chance to take FOUR more specially selected titles from the Medical Romance™ series absolutely FREE! We're also making this offer to introduce you to the benefits of the Reader Service™—

- ★ FREE home delivery
- ★ FREE gifts and competitions
- ★ FREE monthly Newsletter
- ★ Books available before they're in the shops
- ★ Exclusive Reader Service discounts

Accepting these FREE books and gift places you under no obligation to buy; you may cancel at any time, even after receiving your free shipment. Simply complete your details below and return the entire page to the address below. *You don't even need a stamp!*

YES! Please send me 4 free Medical Romance books and a surprise gift. I understand that unless you hear from me, I will receive 6 superb new titles every month for just £2.49 each, postage and packing free. I am under no obligation to purchase any books and may cancel my subscription at any time. The free books and gift will be mine to keep in any case.

MIZEB

Ms/Mrs/Miss/Mr ....Initials................................
BLOCK CAPITALS PLEASE

Surname ....

Address ....

....

....Postcode ....

Send this whole page to:
UK: The Reader Service, FREEPOST CN81, Croydon, CR9 3WZ
EIRE: The Reader Service, PO Box 4546, Kilcock, County Kildare (stamp required)

Offer not valid to current Reader Service subscribers to this series. We reserve the right to refuse an application and applicants must be aged 18 years or over. Only one application per household. Terms and prices subject to change without notice. Offer expires 31st May 2002. As a result of this application, you may receive offers from other carefully selected companies. If you would prefer not to share in this opportunity please write to The Data Manager at the address above.

Mills & Boon® is a registered trademark owned by Harlequin Mills & Boon Limited.
Medical Romance™ is being used as a trademark.